"Do you have any idea what
you're doing to me?
I used to be an even-tempered guy,
with an uncomplicated life..."

"Long time ago, in a galaxy far, far away." She tried to strike a casual pose. He gave her a look that said he saw through her pretended indifference.

"Cassie, you're amazing." He shook his head and gazed at her tenderly. "My practice was relatively unexciting until you arrived. You seem to have a distinct knack for attracting the bizarre."

She meant to tell him it wasn't true, that she didn't attract the bizarre. It was just that she'd been having a bout of rotten luck lately. She couldn't explain it; but ever since she'd met him, things had been going wrong. She meant to tell him this, but his eyes held her mesmerizingly, and to her utter dismay she realized she couldn't speak.

Dear Reader:

Last month we were delighted to announce the arrival of TO HAVE AND TO HOLD, the thrilling new romance series that takes you into the world of married love. This month we're pleased to report that letters of praise and enthusiasm are pouring in daily. TO HAVE AND TO HOLD is clearly off to a great start!

TO HAVE AND TO HOLD is the first and only series that portrays the joys and heartaches of marriage. Its unique concept makes it significantly different from the other lines now available to you, and it offers stories that meet the high standards set by SECOND CHANCE AT LOVE. TO HAVE AND TO HOLD offers all the compelling romance, exciting sensuality, and heartwarming entertainment you expect.

We think you'll love TO HAVE AND TO HOLD—and that you'll become the kind of loyal reader who is making SECOND CHANCE AT LOVE an ever-increasing success. Read about love affairs that last a lifetime. Look for three TO HAVE AND TO HOLD romances each and every month, as well as six SECOND CHANCE AT LOVE romances each month. We hope you'll read and enjoy them all. And please keep writing! Your thoughts about our books are very important to us.

Warm wishes,

Ellen Edwards

Ellen Edwards
SECOND CHANCE AT LOVE
The Berkley Publishing Group
200 Madison Avenue
New York, N.Y. 10016

THE LOVING TOUCH
AIMÉE DUVALL

SECOND CHANCE AT LOVE
BOOK

*With special thanks to
Susan Flenniken, Dr. Bret Snyder,
and Dr. Tim McKenna.*

*But especially to Dr. Mary Hume,
because it never happened to her.*

THE LOVING TOUCH

CHAPTER
One

WITH A FEELING of anticipation Cassie Prentiss got inside her VW bug and slammed the door shut. The black vinyl seat, dried and worn by the desert sun, crackled as she settled herself comfortably behind the wheel. The motor turned over with a satisfying roar, and she pulled out into the street.

The sun was high in a bright, cloudless sky. The desert countryside, dotted with sagebrush and cactus, looked radiant on this warm spring day. As she drove down familiar streets, glimpsing flat-roofed adobe houses, Cassie's thoughts turned to money . . . and men.

Her financial situation had become intolerable. A sim-

ple miscalculation in her income-tax computations (she'd
failed to carry down a zero, the IRS agent had told her)
was now costing her dearly. Instead of owing Uncle Sam
two hundred dollars, she owed two thousand!

Unfortunately, by the time she got the news, she had
already quit her job at the Town and Country Animal
Clinic. Her throat tightened with anxiety as she recalled
the painful situation she'd been involved in there. As
associates of the aging Dr. Kline, she and Craig Brown-
low had worked together for the past five years. During
that time Cassie had fallen head over heels in love with
him. Craig had seemed to return her feelings, but his
inability to make a commitment had doomed their relationship. She had needed much more than the carefree,
on again—off again friendship he had been willing to
offer. To her mind, what they felt for each other should
lead naturally to a ring on her finger, a home in the
suburbs, and a baby on the way. But Craig had viewed
marriage as the end of freedom, and he was not about
to make that sacrifice—not for her or any other woman.
Feeling hurt and betrayed, Cassie had resigned her job
and set about seeking a fresh start elsewhere.

Now she had the chance she'd been hoping for. She
was on her way to interview for a position as assistant
veterinarian at the well-known Albuquerque City Zoo.

Stopping at a traffic light, she glanced at the rearview
mirror and freshened her lipstick. Her wispy, coal-black
bangs shone in the sunlight and complemented her richly
tanned skin. Scrutinizing her appearance, she stared into
the dark emerald eyes reflecting back at her. She hoped
she looked the perfect candidate for the job: feminine,
but not frail; competent, but not hard.

The blare of a car horn behind her announced that the

light had turned green. Stepping on the accelerator, she drove past a large billboard depicting snakes and gorillas, advertising the zoo whose gates she was approaching. Her hands were clammy with nervous perspiration as she turned into the grounds and began searching for a parking space.

The area reserved for staff was already filled with cars. She was about to give up and head for the regular parking lot when she spotted a narrow opening between a large luxury van and a small gray sports car. It would be a tight squeeze, but she could make it.

Shifting into low gear, she began to inch her car forward. The angle of her approach made entry difficult, particularly on the far side, where there was almost no clearance between her bug and the van. Careful to maintain a few inches between them, she proceeded slowly. Then, as she looked up to verify that the path ahead was clear, she saw the most spectacular-looking man she had ever laid eyes on. Standing almost directly in front of her, he was slightly over six feet tall, with a lean frame that supported a firm but not overly muscular build. Rich brown hair cascaded over his forehead, and his tanned face was set off by a strong jaw and an uncompromising mouth. He was fishing something out of his pocket when she caught his eye and flashed him a glowing smile.

At that very instant her car lurched forward and the sickening crunch of metal scraping against metal brought her back to earth with a thud. The little sports car on her left rocked violently as her fender made contact with it. Too late, she pulled her car away from it and killed the motor.

"Damn!" The way her luck was going, it was probably *his* car. A quick glance at his horrified expression confirmed her suspicions. Covering her face with one hand, she let out a deep breath. She should have stayed home today.

"Lady, what do you think you're doing? For the love of Pete! Look what you've done!" He ran to the front of his car, his expression forbidding. "This must be my punishment for leaving the City Council meeting early."

Unfastening her seat belt, Cassie prepared to face the consequences. She tried to push open her door, but it wouldn't budge. Now what? She had to get out of the car. She hurled her shoulder against the door, and it flew open, smashing into the side of the sports car.

The man turned away, groaning. "By the time you get through I'm going to need a vacuum cleaner to pick up what's left of my car!"

Cassie wished she could vanish into thin air. She got out of the VW and approached him hesitantly. He was dressed in a khaki jumpsuit that sported the zoo's emblem over the right shoulder pocket. Hands on hips, he stood braced with his feet apart. His cornflower-blue eyes sparkled with icy fire, but even his hostility, obvious as it was, failed to diminish his physical effect on her. There was a subtle arrogance about him that left her tongue-tied, self-conscious, and very sensually aware.

"I'm so sorry!" she stammered, uncertain of how to deal with his anger. She tried a tentative smile. "At least no one's been hurt."

His eyes remained cold with rage. "That's no plus as far as I'm concerned." His steely gaze swept over her, from head to toe and back up again. She got the distinct impression that he was sizing her up, searching for telltale signs of mental incompetency.

Trying to sound confident and reassuring, but suspecting she sounded neither, Cassie said, "The damage to your car doesn't look extensive. We'll call the police, have them file a report, and then I'll contact my insurance company. I'm sure we can fix it up in no time."

He edged sideways between their vehicles and inspected his fender, muttering a soft curse. Carefully he opened the door, slipped behind the wheel, and started the motor. As he began edging out of the parking space, the already loosened side trim fell to the ground with a loud clang. Cassie cringed.

Ignoring both her and the fallen part, the man drove a few yards away and parked in front of the administration building. Cassie picked up the shiny metal strip and offered it to him. "Here. This came off when you started to pull away." At the venomous look on his face, she took an involuntary step backward, wishing she could slink away and find a nice dark hole to hide in. Maybe if she prayed really hard the ground would swallow her whole.

"Thanks," he muttered sarcastically. "I always did like this trim. Of course, I liked it a lot better when it was part of my car." Cassie shifted uncomfortably under his unswerving stare. "You realize, of course, that you're not even supposed to be here," he went on. "This area is reserved for staff members only." He jammed his hands into the pockets of his jumpsuit and glowered at her.

"The woman who called me from administration told me to park here." Cassie inhaled deeply and with a burst of courage, challenged his stony glare. For a moment she felt as if she were drowning in the deep blue eyes that sparkled like sunlight on ocean waves. Why couldn't she have met him under more favorable circumstances!

"Someone actually invited you here?" he asked in disbelief, brushing a shock of hair out of his eyes.

She conceded that he had a right to be upset, but his

rudeness was making her angry. "Look, mister, it was an accident. I'm just as sorry as you are that it happened. My car's not exactly unscathed, you know. I suggest you calm down. Being unpleasant isn't going to help matters one bit."

He looked away from her, his hands tightening into fists at his sides. Then he took a deep breath and pressed his lips together. Although he wasn't quite succeeding, he seemed to be genuinely trying to suppress his temper. Cassie held his gaze and smiled hesitantly. "I'll be glad to cover any of the damages. My deductible is rather high, so I'm certain my insurance company isn't going to be much help. But please don't worry. If the repairs turn out to be more than I can afford, then we can either work out payments..." Sensing his impatience, she sighed. "I'm sorry. I always babble when I'm nervous. Did you want to say something?"

Surprisingly, his lips formed a seductive half-smile, and his voice held a hint of mockery as he said, "You've ruined my car, you've ruined my day. Is there anything else you'd like to do to me and my car while I'm still here? Slash my tires? Steal my tape deck? Smash in the windshield? I'm sure you—"

"Paul!" He stopped in mid-sentence, and Cassie looked up to see a blonde wearing a dark blue corduroy pants suit emerge from the administration building. "Paul, we've got your overseas call. Jacques Dupree is on the line."

Groaning, he shot Cassie another black look. "I have to get that. Stay here."

"I can't," she blurted, embarrassed because she couldn't even do that much for him. "I'm really not trying to be difficult, but I'm already late for my appointment." She scribbled her name and telephone number on a piece of notepaper. "I'll be around here for a while. Ask someone in administration to find me if you need my driver's license or my signature on any reports for the police. Here's my home phone number. I'll be there tonight for sure; so if you'll give me a call, we can work out the details then. I'll have your car fixed in no time, I promise."

"Paul!" the woman called again.

With a nod, he took the paper from Cassie's hand, shoved it into his breast pocket, and ran toward the building.

As he disappeared inside, Cassie felt a twinge of disappointment. Heaving a sigh, she leaned against one of the parked cars. She was acting like an idiot. Meeting an attractive stranger usually brought out the best in her, but today she was as clumsy as a two-day-old puppy. What was wrong with her?

Reluctantly, she shifted her thoughts back to the business at hand. She retrieved her medical bag from the back seat of the VW and hurried across the parking lot. She probably wouldn't need her instruments today, but her readiness to begin work immediately might impress her interviewer. And considering how late she was, she would need all the help she could get. She had to get this job!

Cassie entered the main office and walked to the receptionist's desk. "Hello, I'm Dr. Prentiss."

"Hello Doctor, I'm Mrs. Ryan. Dr. Kelly was asking for you earlier." The woman smiled and paused obviously expecting an explanation.

"I had a small problem parking," Cassie said.

The receptionist gave her a quizzical look and pressed the intercom buzzer. No one answered. "Dr. Kelly doesn't seem to be at his desk, but I know he's expecting you.

Why don't you go on back there and wait? His office is directly through those doors and to your right. You can't miss it. I'm sure he'll be back in no time."

Cassie nodded. "Thank you."

As she walked down the hall, she tried to look confident, though her stomach was tied in knots. Realizing how badly she needed the work made her even more nervous. Despite all the mishaps so far, she would have to collect herself and make an absolutely unforgettable impression on Dr. Kelly. She just *had* to convince him that she was the ideal candidate for the job! Only one thought nagged at her. Judging from the year and model of the car she had hit, its owner was a man of some importance. He might even be a trustee. But would a trustee wear the zoo's khaki jumpsuit? She relaxed. It didn't matter. With any luck Dr. Kelly would never hear of the incident, at least not until after he had hired her as his assistant.

She pushed open the swinging double doors and entered the hospital area. Shrill animal cries blended into a chaotic symphony around her. Finding the door marked P. Kelly, D.V.M., she strolled inside. The tiny, congested room was in a state of disarray. Folders in need of filing were piled high on top of a gray metal desk as well as on the windowsill. The walls were lined with shelves, some merely rough boards propped up on bricks. A wooden table with chipped white paint stood in one corner and was almost completely covered by stacks of papers.

Searching for a seat, Cassie moved a wire basket full of medical journals from a chair that she surmised was intended for visitors and, after clearing a corner of the desk, set it down beside a wooden marker that read:

SECOND VICE-PRESIDENT
in charge of all vice

At least Dr. Kelly had a sense of humor. Making herself comfortable, she sat down to wait.

CHAPTER
Two

TWENTY MINUTES LATER, Cassie decided to seek out Dr. Kelly. From a brief exchange with a lab volunteer she learned that he'd last been seen heading for the camel enclosure. Determined to find him, she left the building.

As she strolled down a pathway that weaved through the park, Cassie enjoyed her few minutes alone. The grounds seemed oddly silent this weekday afternoon, with children in school and parents at work. Yet she knew that, come the weekend, the walks would be filled with families trying to catch glimpses of the zoo's inhabitants.

The seventy-acre zoo housed a variety of mammals

and reptiles. Dry moats and low concrete walls separated the visitors from the enclosures while at the same time providing the best possible views.

Special pains had been taken to display each species in an environment as close to its natural habitat as possible. The giraffes were housed in an area resembling the African savanna. The rhinos, usually found in temperate grasslands, were provided with large mud puddles in which to wallow, an enormous pool of water, and several shade trees.

Cassie was well aware that although this zoo was not considered particularly large, it had acquired a reputation for excellence. She noticed that each exhibit was meticulously maintained, and she surmised that each animal was kept in the best possible health through a program of preventive medicine.

Stopping to get her bearings, she spotted three men dressed in the khaki jumpsuits and parkas worn by zoo employees conferring in the front of the camel enclosure. Two of them were looking over the low wall while the third straddled the barrier, viewing the camels through field glasses.

A freckle-faced young man greeted her as she approached. "Can we help you, ma'am?"

"I'm Dr. Prentiss, here to see Dr. Kelly."

"I've been expecting you, Doctor," the man on the wall replied, not turning around. He continued to observe the animals. "Stick around. You might learn something."

The hair at the back of Cassie's neck stood on end as she recognized the voice. Hardly breathing, she waited for him to turn around, praying her guess was wrong. Nervously, her eyes darted to the oldest member of the trio, who had not yet spoken. The deep lines that etched his face attested to many years of outdoor work. There was a rugged, weather-beaten quality about him. He cleared his throat. "I'm Mac." Pointing to the sandy-haired youth by his side, he added, "And this is Joey, my assistant."

Cassie gave him a shaky smile. "Nice to meet you both."

The man straddling the barrier placed the binoculars on the wall next to him, swung his leg over the wall, and jumped to the ground. "By the way, Dr. Prentiss, you're late."

It didn't take more than a glimpse of his profile for her to confirm his identity. For Paul Kelly, however, recognition came as a total shock. Wide-eyed, he inhaled sharply and took a quick step backward, brushing against the field glasses and knocking them over the edge. They tumbled down the incline.

"Not you again!" Dr. Kelly groaned. "First you destroy my car, and now thanks to you I've lost my binoculars!"

Cassie hurried forward and spotted the field glasses lying directly below them.

"Don't worry, I'll get them for you. They don't look broken." Not giving Dr. Kelly a chance to protest, she rested her stomach on the wall and leaned forward as far as she could. The strap was only inches from her fingertips.

She strained to close the gap, yet maintain her balance. Suddenly her body slipped. She gave a startled yelp as she slid over the retaining wall and toppled onto the soft sand below. For a moment she just lay there, wishing that, like an ostrich, she could simply bury her head. Then, realizing she was unhurt, she stood up and wiped the dust from her face. She glanced up to see all three men staring down at her.

Dr. Kelly appeared to be seriously concerned, but even from this distance she could tell that his eyes held a hint of amusement. Standing on either side of Dr. Kelly, the curator Mac and his assistant Joey peered down at her with the curiosity one might reserve for an ugly but fascinating insect.

Trying to regain some measure of dignity, Cassie stood at the base of the wall and squared her shoulders. "May I have a hand up, Dr. Kelly?" she requested calmly.

He encircled her wrist easily in a strong grip. Gaining confidence from the strength of his grasp, she pulled hard and began to scale the wall.

"Wait a minute," he called. "I need to get a better hold on the—" Whatever he'd been about to say ended in a strangled gasp as she pulled him off his narrow perch, and he came crashing toward her. His body knocked her aside and they tumbled to the sand in a tangle of arms and legs.

Shaking his head as if trying to clear his brain, Kelly sat up slowly.

"I . . ." Cassie's throat constricted with humiliation. What could she say? How could she explain that she was simply having the worst day of her entire life?

"Are you hurt?" Dr. Kelly asked, moving his leg from between hers and pulling her away from his chest, where for a brief moment she'd been comfortably nestled.

"I'm fine." She glanced at him quickly and almost gasped at the smoldering look in his eyes. "Are you?"

"Yes." He ran a hand through his hair, pushing it off his face. "If I bribe you, can I get you to stay away from me?" He sounded both resigned and amused.

Cassie's face burned. "I'm so embarrassed! I don't even know what to—" She stopped abruptly as a loud hissing came from close behind her.

"Don't move," Paul warned.

Cassie froze. Suddenly she remembered where she was: in a camel enclosure. Just as suddenly she remembered having read that camels could be notoriously mean when angered.

At that moment Mac appeared at the back gate leading into the exhibit. "I've got the CO_2 gun, Doc," he whispered harshly. "How much sedative should I use to knock out the animals?"

"How many are behind me?" Cassie asked, breaking out in a cold sweat.

Dr. Kelly gave a quick glance. "There are two camels in this enclosure. They're not mean, just cranky. Keep cool and we'll be just fine." He looked at Mac. "It'll take me a minute or two since I have to move very slowly, but keep the gun and the tranquilizer vial there for me. I'll take care of it myself."

As he started to rise, the larger camel immediately screeched and ran toward them. From Cassie's seated position the seven-foot-tall animal looked especially imposing.

In an incredible burst of energy, Paul leaped to his feet and yanked Cassie up with him. Pushing her away from him with all his might, he began flailing his arms and yelling at the top of his lungs, drawing both camels' attention toward him. He was sprinting across the pen when one of the animals lunged, closing the gap between them. Craning its neck, it shut its massive jaws around the edge of Paul's parka and shook its head, shredding the material to bits. Thrown forward, Paul landed on his hands and knees.

Within seconds Cassie was at his side. Pulling him up while the other men entered the pen and tried to distract the camels, she grasped Dr. Kelly's hand and began running as fast as she could toward the gate. Just then the large male camel cut across the enclosure and emerged in front of them, blocking their escape. Cassie turned in mid-stride and sped off in the opposite direction. With a sinking sensation she realized that she and Dr. Kelly were trapped in the corner with no place to run. Quickly they exchanged questioning glances. Simultaneously, they dove toward the chain-link fence bordering the back of the enclosure and scrambled up and over it. Cassie hit the ground with a numbing thud.

As they reached safety, the curator and his assistant made a hasty retreat from the pen and hurried over to them.

"Doc, are you all right?" Mac asked.

"Yes, I'm fine." Leaning over, hands on his knees, Dr. Kelly paused to recover his breath.

"How the hell did you two end up in there?" The curator looked aghast.

"We have Dr. Prentiss to thank for that." Dr. Kelly straightened his massive frame, towering over Cassie.

"It was an accident," she croaked. "I'm really sorry. I'm not usually so clumsy." She wanted to cry or scream, perhaps do both. Her cheeks burned as her eyes met his. He looked so confident and self-assured! Despite her determination not to, she felt intimidated. Valiantly she tried to salvage what was left of her self-esteem. After all, this was supposed to be a job interview! "I know what you must think," she said more firmly, "but I'm really a very competent professional. For the past four years I've worked in a clinic that specialized in farm animals, and my references are excellent. I'm a hard worker, and I always give each and every task my very best."

"Oh, I won't argue with that." For the first time Paul

Kelly smiled. His features softened, and his eyes seemed to light up with a roguish gleam.

Her heart leaped. His gaze was focused solely on her, and for a brief moment she felt as if she were the only person in the entire world who merited his attention. She was flattered yet oddly disturbed by his scrutiny. He certainly was handsome!

What was the matter with her? She needed this job desperately, yet here she was entertaining these incredibly unprofessional thoughts! "What I meant was..."

His stance and expression told her he had sensed her reaction to him and was deriving enormous pleasure from it.

Suddenly she was determined to dispel any such notion from his mind. "Well, at least this time we came out even."

He blinked. "Even? How do you figure that?"

"You helped by pushing me out of the way when the camel charged, and I helped when you fell down. That makes us even."

"You're forgetting that it was you who knocked me in there in the first place."

"Oh." She stopped short. Her eyes focused on the zipper of his jumpsuit, which had worked its way downward, exposing a patch of dark, curly hair. She found herself wondering what he'd look like bare-chested. As her eyes returned to his face, she caught his mocking grin. Averting her gaze quickly, she tried to hide her embarrassment by taking an unexpected gambit. "I suppose this means you're not going to give my application a fair chance."

He stared at her in surprise. "Now wait a minute—"

"That's really too bad...for both of us." Knowing

she had nothing to lose by being bold, and motivated by visions of dire poverty, she gave him a slow, disappointed smile. "Believe it or not, I'm one heck of a good vet. If nothing else, this incident with the camels should prove that I can keep my head in an emergency." She sighed. "I'd really like to work here, Doctor. If you give me a break, I promise you won't regret it. Be fair. Please consider my application. If you decide you still want to interview me, I'll be more than happy to come back at your convenience." She regarded him hopefully, praying he'd ask her to stay.

Suddenly he began laughing. "I don't believe you!"

She pursed her lips and glowered at him. He was insulting her. "I'm sorry you find this all so amusing, Doctor. You'll never know it now, but I could have been the best assistant you ever had!"

She started to turn away, but he grasped her arm. "Wait." She turned to face him. "I had one of the secretaries call the police," he said. "You'll have to be here when they arrive so I can get your license number as well as your signature on the accident report."

"Oh." Her shoulders sagged.

His eyes stayed on her. "Besides, I have to fill you in on your new job."

"What?" Her voice rose expectantly.

Mac was sitting next to Joey on one of the park benches, listening to the exchange. "Doc Kelly, this isn't the same woman you told us about, is it? The one who ran into your car?"

"The one and only, Mac," Paul confirmed.

The curator's eyes lit up. "Doc, are you going to need us to help you with the camels?"

"No, all I wanted to do today was watch the female

and gauge the extent of the problem. I'll come back tomorrow to examine the tumor and remove it."

"In that case, we'll be on our way." Mac nudged his assistant. "Let's go, Joey. We've got work to do."

Cassie watched them leave. "I'd be willing to bet," she ventured slowly, "that within the next thirty minutes everyone's going to know what happened here."

"You're underestimating Mac. I'd say it'll be more like fifteen minutes." Paul laughed. "I'll probably be voted saint of the month if you do end up working here."

Once again her heart fell. "I thought you just offered me the job," she said quietly.

"Let me fill you in on it first; then we'll see if *you're* still interested."

"I'm interested, I'm interested!"

"You don't know anything about it yet."

"I know it's a wonderful challenge. I realize your impression of me is something less than awe-inspiring; but if you hire me, I guarantee that within a month you'll wonder how you ever did without me."

He laughed. "You have the gift of prophecy, do you?" He picked up his medical bag. "Come on. We'll have to walk back to the hospital. I didn't bother to bring the ambulance with me."

As she fell into step beside him, Cassie felt an incredible surge of excitement. There was an irresistible vitality about Dr. Kelly. She found herself wondering what he thought of her. Did he find her attractive? Did she affect him the way he affected her? She flinched inwardly, hating herself for even considering such questions. She'd just left a job because she'd gotten too emotionally involved with the man she worked with. As they walked, she tried to study Paul Kelly in quick unobtrusive glimpses. He was, after all, only a man—a tall, incredibly handsome man with the most devastating eyes and the most captivating smile . . .

"Do you know anything about zoo practice?" he asked abruptly.

"Not much, but I can learn," she replied quickly.

He chuckled. "I think I better take out more insurance. The way things are going, I'll probably end up in traction." His voice was deep and very masculine. Its throaty timbre had a seductive quality.

"I'm very easy to work with, Dr. Kelly, and I'm an excellent diagnostician."

"Not to mention a modest one." As they crossed the compound, Cassie struggled to keep up with his long strides.

Using the back entrance, they headed for his office. He stepped aside and waved her in. "Have a seat . . . Shall I call you Cassandra?"

"Call me Cassie, please." She sat down opposite him. "I think Cassandra sounds like a good name for a horse."

"Whatever you say."

As their eyes locked, she felt the force of his penetrating gaze. Blood raced through her veins as she concentrated on presenting a businesslike facade. What was it about this man that made her feel weak in the knees? She felt a sexual tension about him that charged the very air around them. Cassie licked her lips, more unsure of herself than ever. His eyes seemed to caress her as they roamed over her body. Chiding herself for having an overactive imagination, she forced her thoughts back to the interview.

"Zoo work is not like private practice, Cassie, as I'm sure you realize now," he said. "Mistakes can be dangerous. The hours are long and the pay is low. Private practice is much more lucrative. I realize that you were only an associate at the animal clinic, but in a few years you'd have developed a strong clientele of your own. You would have been able to open your own office, and then your earnings would have exceeded anything we could pay you here by four or five times."

"I know I'd enjoy the challenge of working here. Money's not the most important consideration in my life," she answered honestly. "It never has been and it never will be." But, she added silently, it sure would be nice to be able to pay her bills!

He nodded. "Let me tell you a little about the way things run around here." She nodded. "Our hierarchy is very simple. First we have the curators. These are the officials who oversee everything involving the major departments of our zoo and make all decisions concerning their areas of responsibility. Mac is our curator of mammals, John Major is curator of reptiles, and Kevin O'Reilly is curator of birds. Each of these men has an assistant. You've already met Joey, Mac's assistant. You'll soon meet the others during the course of your work."

She *did* have the job! The realization made it impossible for her to suppress a tiny, triumphant grin.

He gave her a knowing smile. "Now then," he continued, "the keepers are usually assigned to a specific group of animals. They maintain close, daily contact with their charges, looking after their physical health as well as taking care of the enclosures. The keepers are supervised by animal managers and assistant animal managers."

She swallowed, hoping she'd remember all this later.

"I know it's a lot of information, but you'll understand the system in no time at all." He walked to the window. "As you've no doubt surmised, we don't have a large operating budget. Our facilities are adequate, but by no means luxurious. For a while, at least, you'll have to share my office. It'll be cramped, but I'm sure we can manage. The one vacant room we had has now been converted into a clinical pathology laboratory. We needed one badly. The labs in town are overloaded with work and whatever we sent them was given low priority. That caused no end of trouble for us."

She'd be working in the small office with him. The prospect excited as well as scared her.

"Come over here," he said. "I want you to see something."

She moved to his side at the window. In one fluid motion, he draped his arm over her shoulders and pulled her against him. Pointing with one hand, he leaned toward her. "You see that small building across the way?"

She nodded. His arm felt warm against her skin. Instinctively, she stepped closer to him, then, aware of what she'd done, moved quickly away.

He gave her a lopsided grin. "Do I make you nervous?"

"No."

"You're acting nervous," he teased.

"I am not!"

"Then come back here so I can point out a few things to you. I promise not to do anything you don't want me to do."

Her hands felt cold and clammy. What was he suggesting? And what in the world had gotten into her? With a curt nod, she returned to his side.

"That building is our quarantine area," he explained. "We follow normal procedure, but I want to emphasize how important it is that we adhere to the rules—like sterilizing the instruments immediately after using them and taking special care not to take any equipment in or out of that area. If for some reason you feel you must break that rule, always clear it with me first. It's imperative that we don't make any mistakes. An epidemic could wipe out most of our animals."

"I understand." She started to return to her seat, but his arm held her steady.

"Wait a minute, will you. Why are you in such a hurry?"

She tried to moisten her lips, but her tongue was dry. "I'm not. I simply thought you had finished."

"You look like you're ready to jump out of your skin." His voice was soft and soothing.

She glanced up, intending to challenge him, to break the spell he was casting over her, but the instant she met his eyes she found herself growing acutely aware of her body, and his. They were too close. She should step back, yet she stood immobile, transfixed by the clear blue eyes that studied her so incisively. She trembled, instinctively knowing what was to come yet incapable of stopping it.

Leaning closer to her, he narrowed the gap between them. His mouth was inches away, and he was looking at her as if trying to memorize every detail of her face. "There's something bewitching about you," he said softly, warm breath caressing her face.

Her heart pounded as newly awakened need coursed through her. She forced herself to remember where she was. Kissing her boss, no matter how pleasant that might be, was definitely a bad idea!

Wondering about her sanity, she slipped gently out of his reach and sat down in a chair. She wouldn't lower her guard again. Paul Kelly was going to be her boss, nothing more. Trying to project an image of poise and calm, she leaned back in her seat and crossed her legs. She would pretend this had never happened.

"Dr. Kelly, I want this job, make no mistake about it, but if you think—"

"You're right. What almost happened...shouldn't have." He gave her an arrogant smile. "Not on city time anyway." He returned to his desk.

She debated whether or not to tell him that such a thing would *never* happen again—before, during, or after work. Finally she decided to let her actions speak for her. "Let's get back to what you were telling me," she suggested.

"I forgot where I left off." The tiny, mocking twist in his mouth suggested that he did remember and was simply testing her, curious to see how strongly he'd affected her.

Cassie tried to recollect their conversation. The only thing she could remember clearly was the intoxicating and passionate promise his lips had held out to her. "I believe you were showing me the quarantine area."

He chuckled. "I mean before that."

She forced herself to concentrate. "You had finished telling me about the different jobs held by the zoo staff. Wait. You had just told me, Dr. Kelly, that we were going to have to share this office." Realizing the import of her words, particularly in view of the tension between them, she felt a warm flush spread over her cheeks.

He appeared not to notice. "Since we go by first names around here, Cassie, you might as well start calling me Paul."

"Paul." She nodded.

"Cassie, I'm going to hire you because something tells me you really need this job and that you'll work hard at it, but I want to know a bit more about you." He opened the manila folder on his desk. "I have all the essentials here on your application. What I'd like you to tell me is the little things that I'd never find out from the questionnaire. For instance, how did you get interested in veterinary practice?"

She tried to answer his questions honestly, but a tiny voice at the back of her mind warned that his interest transcended their business relationship. "I've always loved being around animals," she said. "To be able to be with them and earn a living at the same time seemed ideal. I never could see myself doing anything else."

He nodded. "You're single?"

"Yes."

"Do you live here in the city or on the outskirts of town?"

"I live in Corrales, just outside the city. It takes me about twenty to twenty-five minutes to get here."

"I'll be honest with you. You've shown a great deal of enthusiasm for the job, and that's a big plus in your favor. I have only one very serious reservation. I'm not sure you realize what you're getting into."

"I beg your pardon?"

"The fact is that zoo practice is an extremely demanding job. A mean dog is tamer than any animal we treat here."

"I realize that, Paul. In fact, it's the challenge that attracts me to this work."

"I'm afraid you're romanticizing the situation. It's hard, dirty work. Days rarely end as planned. A five-day week more often than not turns into a six- or seven-day marathon. There'll be times when you won't even get home—you'll have to sleep here at the hospital. If you have a steady boyfriend, you can just about forget seeing him on any kind of regular basis."

"I don't have a boyfriend." Inwardly Cassie cringed. How could she have let that information slip out? It was none of his business.

He gave her a maddening smile, then continued. "Your job here is going to encroach on your spare time. You'd never have that problem in a private practice, where you can always send clients to the emergency animal clinics that are open after hours."

"I'm sure you manage to have a personal life and still work here," she countered. "I can too. If your wife or girl friend can put up with the hours, then I'll have to find someone who will too."

There was a pause. "My wife died two years ago," he finally said quietly. The pain in his eyes made Cassie's heart constrict. "And I don't have a girl friend."

She found it difficult to breathe. Why had she opened her big mouth? She had a remarkable talent for saying the wrong thing at the wrong time! There was a knot at the back of her throat as she fumbled for the right words. "I didn't realize . . . I'm sorry . . . I . . ." She stopped, trying to convey with her eyes what she couldn't put into words.

"Your apology isn't necessary, Cassie." He smiled gently. "Fair's fair."

His words calmed her, but only for a split second before she realized what was happening: this man, who she had known only two hours, had the power to soothe, enrage, even entice her with only a few words. Paul Kelly was without a doubt the most dangerous man she had ever met.

Trying to steel herself against him, she tossed her head back in a defiant gesture before meeting his gaze. "I know what I'm getting into by accepting this job, Paul. I also know what I want. My only question is, why are you trying to talk me out of it?"

"Because I don't want to spend the next six months training you and then have you quit because it wasn't what you expected. And because I have a sneaking suspicion you have no idea what you're letting yourself in for. Today was a good example of what can happen here."

"Obviously I'm no worse for wear. That should prove something to you."

He shook his head. "What about the animals we can't tranquilize before treatment? The CO_2 gun is handy, but there are species we can't use it on. You've seen those cute little seals at the edge of the compound? Our darts won't penetrate their thick layer of fat. But underneath that, they're ninety percent muscle. They'll toss someone your size around like a rubber ball if you try to restrain them. I don't relish the thought of having to sweep up what's left of you."

"I'm much stronger than I look."

"You're what"—he paused to appraise her with a look that sent her pulse soaring—"about five-foot-four and a hundred and ten pounds? You don't stand a chance."

The thoroughness of his gaze made her shift uncomfortably in her seat. "I'm young and I have a lot more stamina and strength than you give me credit for. I'll manage." Cassie met his blue eyes without flinching.

He referred back to the manila folder and said, "You're twenty-eight." He seemed to guess her thoughts as he added, "I'm thirty-five."

She tore her eyes from his gaze and looked around the room again. She hated being so transparent. "What about my duties?"

"Basically, they're whatever I tell you to do. For now, you'll be working as my assistant. Later on, when you're more familiar with our procedures, we'll split our rounds in half and each take different sections."

"All right." Working with him wouldn't be easy. What was it about this man that left her feeling vulnerable and incredibly feminine? She looked away. She must be losing her mind, that's all there was to it. If she didn't need the job so much, she'd run as fast as she could from a situation that seemed to be growing more dangerous by the minute.

"During your first six months you'll be on probation," Paul continued. "If by the end of that time you're still around, you'll have the opportunity to become a permanent member of our staff."

"You really don't think I'm going to make it, do you?"

"I have some doubts, but I think you're a good risk." He walked around the desk and, leaning against the front, crossed his arms over his chest. "Don't disappoint me."

She clenched her jaw, suddenly angry because he was so arrogantly self-confident while she was fighting emotions that left her extremely insecure.

"You'll need to pick up a few khaki jumpsuits," he went on. "Any of the larger department stores should carry them. There's no rush, but the sooner you get them the better off you'll be. Clothing can take quite a beating around here." He handed her several zoo patches. "Sew these onto your uniforms."

She nodded. "Fine. What time do you want me to come in to work each morning, and where do you want me to park?" She was trying to keep her words and her tone impersonal, but the current of sensual awareness between them was too strong. She felt as if she were being swept away toward an inescapable destiny, one that would bring her only harm.

"Report to work at nine in the morning. We'll start

our rounds then. As for parking, I'll try to see that you have a space the size of Wyoming set aside for you." His tone dripped with sarcasm. "Now that you know my car—and with the souvenir you left on the side of it, you should be able to pick it out easily—*stay away from it!*"

She was repeating her offer to pay for the repairs, when a light knock on the door interrupted her. She turned to see a statuesque blonde wearing an immaculate white linen suit standing in the doorway.

Smiling, the woman stepped inside. "Hello, Paul." She turned toward Cassie and extended her hand. "And you must be Cassandra Prentiss."

"Call me Cassie, please." Standing next to this woman, she felt as appealing as a wilted daisy.

"I'm Debbie Stewart. I take care of public relations."

Paul smiled. "She's being modest. Debbie *is* our public relations department. Without her, nothing would ever run right around here."

The woman chuckled and gave Cassie a knowing look. "If he's being nice to me, I'd better watch out. Last time he was this cordial I ended up organizing a fund-raising drive so he could get a new cardiac monitoring machine."

Cassie laughed.

Debbie's attention focused on Paul once again. "I'm going to need you to go over a few details of your report for me. I want to make sure of the facts before we go to the board of directors tomorrow."

Paul nodded. "Cassie, why don't you go home and get some rest—you've had a long day! I'll be in a meeting tomorrow morning. While I'm there, you can take a look at the zebras. Mac said one of them was limping. You've treated horses before, haven't you?" She nodded.

"Good. It'll be easy for you then. I'll leave all the information you'll need as well as the keys to the enclosure on my desk."

"Fine."

"Take the zoo's ambulance. It's the pickup parked at the back. It's clearly marked, so you can't miss it. Everything you'll need for a field examination is stored in the cabinets in the back. Do you think you can handle it without me?"

Eager to prove her worth, she nodded and smiled confidently. "No problem at all."

He paused as if considering a question, then said, "You have driven a truck before, haven't you?"

"Oh, of course! Whenever I made house calls to any of the farms I used the truck at the clinic." She tried to sound confident, hoping he'd forget about the accident that had left his car looking like a potato chip with ridges.

"All right," he said, though he still looked doubtful. "If you run into any problems, or if you're unsure about anything, don't hesitate to come and get me. I'll be in the conference room at the other end of the building."

"Will do." She stood up.

"See you tomorrow afternoon then."

As Cassie walked outside, she was filled with apprehension. She had the job, but, now it was up to her to prove her worth. Could she really handle it? And what about the dangerous attraction she felt for Paul Kelly—could she handle that? She'd have to, she thought with a sigh; she had no choice.

CHAPTER
Three

EXAMINING THE ZEBRAS the next morning turned out to be a lot more complicated than Cassie had expected. Shooting a tranquilizer dart into the colt was easy. But the sedative hadn't had a chance to take full effect before the half-doped colt panicked and bolted into a drainage ditch left open by workmen repairing a sewer line. As she stood thigh-deep in stinking, slimy muck, straining to hold up the animal's heavy head so it wouldn't drown, Cassie tried to tell herself that it was all in the line of duty.

As soon as help arrived to hoist the animal out of the

ditch, Cassie completed her examination. Then she snuck back into the building, hoping no one would see her before she had a chance to clean up. She'd leave Paul a note saying she'd gone home to shower and change.

Although the stench clinging to her clothing would probably make any attempt at concealment futile, she tiptoed down the hallway and paused at each corner, peering cautiously around before going on. Once a man in a white coat stepped into the corridor, and she ducked into a broom closet just in time to avoid him.

Finally she reached Paul's office and sighed with relief. She reached for a pencil and paper and began to scribble a message.

"My, what a wonderful aroma!" Paul's voice boomed from behind her. Startled, she dropped the pencil and whirled around. He was standing in the doorway with his hand over his face. She was utterly humiliated.

Cassie squirmed under his scrutiny and refused to meet his eyes. "I had a bit of a problem with the zebra," she admitted.

His nose twitched, and then unexpectedly he began to laugh. "So you decided to intimidate it by gassing it to death?"

"Paul, don't say another word," she warned. "Not unless you want me to come over and give you a great big hug."

A look of horror replaced all traces of amusement on his face, and he took a step backward. "Tell me what happened."

She'd have gladly given a year's salary not to have him see her like this. Suddenly she felt like crying. "What difference does it make how it happened? It happened."

"Tell me," he insisted.

She sighed. "It's simple, The keeper assured me that the animals would avoid the ditch. He was wrong." She shrugged. "At least I managed to finish the examination. A pebble had lodged in the colt's hoof, forming an abscess. I took care of it."

"Good. Once the animal is down, rule number one around here is to finish the job. Anesthetics are hard on our exotics, and we don't want to subject them to any more trauma than is absolutely necessary."

Cassie felt miserable. "I still can't believe it. Of all the places that zebra could have gone, why did he have to pick the only hazardous area in that entire compound?"

"That's the kind of thing you'll face every day on this job, I'm afraid." Seeing the look in her eye, Paul softened his tone. "Look, it could have happened to any one of us."

"That's easy for you to say," she muttered, pushing a strand of hair away from her face.

He laughed. "Don't worry about it." Watching her pin her hair back, he added, "If I were you, I wouldn't worry about your hairstyle. In view of the rest of you, it's not worth bothering with."

She gave him a sharp look. Had he been a gentleman, he'd have tried to make her feel better, not worse! But she was determined not to let him know how upset she was. "I realize my new perfume, Eau de Excrement, turns you on," she said, "but you really must try to control yourself, Paul. I mean, we have an image to uphold. Imagine what the animals would think if you got carried away!"

"Trust me. You haven't got a thing to worry about." He shook his head. "You'd better go wash up before you get sick."

"I'm going home. I'll be back in an hour or so."

"Wait a minute. You can't stay in those clothes a moment longer. I'm not kidding, Cassie. You're liable to end up really ill. Wash off here, then go home."

"Just one little problem," she said sarcastically, her patience at an end. "Since I don't have any clean clothes handy, what do you suggest I do? Become the zoo's first streaker?"

"I wouldn't mind, but I have a better idea. Wear this." He handed her his trench coat from the hook behind the door and grimaced. "Yech."

"Tell me, Doc, is that a new medical term?"

Ignoring her, he led the way down the hall. "The water-therapy room is on your right. There's a hose in there. Strip, wash off, then give me your clothes so I can burn them. You can wear my trench coat home."

"Very funny."

"I'm not kidding."

"You're forgetting that an observation window comprises half the door. I'd have more privacy on a football field!"

"I'll stand in front of it and make sure no one looks."

"No way!"

He coughed and waved his hand in front of his face. "Please, I'll do anything you ask! Just go take a bath!"

Cassie considered telling him to go play in the tiger cage, but the temptation to get out of her foul clothes was greater. "All right. Go get some towels and cover the window completely."

"You've got it. I'll bring a couple of extra ones for you to dry off with."

Cassie eyed the tiled room with suspicion. There was something terribly undignified about bathing here. Pacing, she waited for Paul to return.

The minute he finished covering the window, she removed her clothing and turned on the water. Twenty minutes later, she returned to his office. His trench coat reached her ankles while the V-neck opening revealed almost as much of her as the length covered up. The wide, triangular gap would have exposed her breasts had she not folded both flaps over and adjusted them to lie closed. Yet even though she knew Paul couldn't see anything, she felt totally naked. "Thanks for the coat," she said, too embarrassed to look directly at him.

"It was no favor. I was just trying to reduce the air pollution. Did you shove your clothes down the incinerator?"

"Of course not. I rinsed them off and left them back in the room. If you have a plastic garbage bag, I'll take them home to wash properly."

"Here—drink this first." He handed her a cup of coffee. "It'll warm you up a bit."

She accepted it gratefully and took a sip. "Thanks."

"I'll be right back."

She breathed a sigh of relief as he left the room. Her hands were still shaking, and not from the cold. As she tugged at the coat, pulling it even tighter around her, she caught the faint scent of lemony after shave clinging to the material. The masculine aroma so close to her own body, tempted her senses. A shiver ran up her spine as the cloth rubbed against her bare breasts. Everything around her, even the clothes she wore, held Paul's mark. She touched her lips, wondering what would have happened yesterday if she hadn't avoided his kiss.

As she focused on his empty chair, she had a sudden feeling that something funny was going on. Where was he? Suspecting the answer, she bolted to her feet and ran down the corridor.

As she turned the corner she saw him closing the incinerator chute. "You didn't!"

"Those clothes were a health hazard. Put in a claim. The zoo will reimburse you."

"How dare you destroy my property!" Her eyes blazed.

"You'd rather have typhoid, I suppose."

She shook her head. "Haven't you ever heard of a washing machine?"

"Even with a ton of disinfectant you still couldn't have been sure. Do you have any idea how many diseases you could contract from the sludge in a sewer? What is it with you? Do you have some kind of death wish?"

She started to retort, but stopped. He had a point. It was better to be safe than sorry. After all, the zoo would reimburse her, and she'd get new clothes out of the deal. "All right, I concede. You win this round."

He gave her a slow smile. "Only this round, huh?"

"Don't press your luck, mister." But her smile softened the words.

Side by side, they returned to his office. "You know," Paul said, "I've been asking for an assistant for the past six years. I finally get one and instead of solving my problems, it seems I've just added a new one."

Despite his light tone, Cassie recoiled inside as if she had just been struck. She couldn't blame him for thinking that, yet his words cut deeply. More than anything, she wanted to earn his trust and respect. "I know I haven't exactly dazzled you with my skills," she said. "Not yet, at least. Still, I want you to know that I'm going to give this job my very best, and I promise that within a few weeks you're going to be glad you hired me. I'm not one to boast, Paul, but I also don't tolerate failure, particularly in myself."

When he smiled, the entire room seemed to light up. "I know you have potential, Cassie."

"I can succeed here too. Just give me a chance to get into the swing of things." Even to her own ears, her voice rang with unmistakable conviction.

"When I hired you, I sensed there was a lot more to you than met the eye. "That's why I overlooked your clumsiness." He raised his hand, stopping her protest. "I still feel that there's a streak of stubbornness in you, a determination that will lead you to accomplish whatever you set out to do." His voice was level, yet it echoed with a seductive timbre that touched her deep inside.

Cassie's cheeks burned. She stared at the dark hairs on the back of his hand. His long fingers, square and strong, had the sensitivity of a skilled surgeon's, and she couldn't help thinking of how it would feel to be touched by them.

Annoyed with herself for the direction her thoughts had taken, she forced them back to business. Paul flashed her a knowing smile. It was almost as if he could read her mind! Thoroughly embarrassed, she reached for the coffee mug and shifted uncomfortably in her chair. Even without looking at him, she knew he was staring at her with the same seductive look that made her knees go weak. She swallowed the rest of her coffee in one long gulp and stood up.

He stood up, too. "I'll drive you home."

"You don't have to. I'm sure I can manage." A slight breeze worked its way beneath the coat, reminding her of her state of undress. Feeling awkward, she tried to jam her hands into the side pockets, but the openings were too low to reach comfortably. Still feeling acutely self-conscious and trying to figure out what to do about it, she worked her arms into the openings of the opposite sleeves and held them against her in a geishalike pose.

"There's really no need for you to be embarrassed." His lips curled in a wicked grin.

She sent him a scathing glance and tried to make light of the situation. "Let's face it, this hasn't been my day. I could have handled a bit of embarrassment. It's the humiliation I'm having trouble with."

He laughed and shook his head, obviously enjoying her discomfiture. "Now don't argue with me, and let me give you a lift to your home in what's left of my car."

"Very funny."

"Don't complain. I'm actually doing you a big favor. If you had to get out of the car for any reason, you could be in trouble."

"I don't see how."

He pointed to the flaps on his coat. "Those have a tendency to come undone."

Cassie stared aghast at her partially exposed breasts. Closing the gap quickly, she kept her hand firmly over the material. "How long has it been that way?" she demanded.

"Actually, I just noticed it."

"Sure you did." There'd been a playfulness in his tone that made it impossible to tell if he was lying.

"Let's go."

Cassie followed Paul outside. While he unlocked his car door, she studied the damaged exterior with a sinking feeling. "I wish I hadn't done that," she murmured.

He slipped into the driver's seat. "Remind me sometime today to work out the details with you."

She nodded miserably. If the repairs turned out to be really expensive, she'd be in big trouble.

As they drove off, Paul said, "I'm going to ask around

and find a reputable firm that does body work. I'll get an estimate and, depending on how much it is, I might just go ahead and have the work done right then. You can pay me back later. Is that all right with you?"

"Fine." What choice did she have? She'd just keep her fingers crossed and hope she could handle the additional strain on her finances.

As they crossed the city and headed into the desert, she noticed that Paul was taking the shortest, most direct route to her house. "You obviously know precisely where you're going, yet I never gave you my address. How do you know where I live?" she asked.

"I looked it up in your file while you were changing."

She shook her head. "But you seem to know exactly which roads to take, even when they're unmarked."

"I live out here too. In fact, my home is the last one before the junction that connects the new interstate highway with the old main road."

"The place with the big adobe wall and gate?" Her eyebrows rose. "You mean you own that big sprawling ranch on Calle Fuego?"

"Guilty as charged, ma'am."

She knew the house well. In fact, she made a point of driving past it at least once a week. It was the kind of spread she dreamed of owning someday. The house itself, nestled in a forest of elms, was absolutely breathtaking. Paul Kelly lived like a king.

Well, one thing was certain. He hadn't acquired that kind of wealth through his job. She glanced at him. He seemed much too down to earth to have been born into wealth. Politeness overruled curiosity and she remained silent, though she continued to speculate.

He turned into the narrow, unpaved street leading to her house and stared at a dilapidated structure in the center of the cul de sac. "What is that, an abandoned house?"

"No, I live there." She chuckled. "Just park in the driveway."

He pulled the car up in front of her garage and got out, standing immobile, gawking at the exterior. "I'm familiar with all sorts of architectural styles in this area, but this . . ." He gestured toward the building. "What is it? Early Devil's Island?"

Cassie laughed. She was delighted with the various reactions people invariably had the first time they saw her home. The gray stucco had crumbled and chipped away in many places, exposing the chicken wire and tar paper underneath. The yard, covered with reddish gravel, looked vaguely like a Martian landscape. "Don't you like my shutters?" She gestured toward the obviously new dark green shutters that framed each window.

He blinked. "They're lovely," he acknowledged, regarding her skeptically.

"I bought them on sale about a month ago."

"If I were you, I'd have saved my money and had the place restuccoed." He gave her an apologetic smile. "Sorry. I didn't mean to criticize."

"It's going to be months before I have the cash to do that. In the meantime, at least I can enjoy my shutters."

"Why would you ever buy a place like this? What did they do, pay you in barley and wheat when you were in private practice?"

"Of course they did!" She laughed again, then explained, "With current market values what they are, I realized I'd never be able to afford a house. Everything was at least ten thousand dollars more than I could finance. Remember, as an associate, I was working strictly on salary. To be honest, I had given up hope when the real estate agent called and told me about this place. It's what they call a Handyman's Special."

"Does it have indoor plumbing?"

She led him toward the front door. "Come in and see for yourself."

He drew in his breath sharply as she guided him inside. "I don't believe it!"

Thick wall-to-wall carpeting covered the floor. The intricately carved wooden and leather furniture had a distinctive Spanish flavor. Navajo rugs hung on the walls. Pottery of Indian design was scattered about the living room, adding to the southwestern ambience. Over all, the look was one of casual elegance.

"I had a roommate for a while," Cassie explained. "By sharing expenses we were able to finish the interior in no time at all. We were just about to start on the exterior when she moved away to get married."

"Did you hire a decorator, or did you two do it all yourselves?" he asked, amazed.

"We did it ourselves. Since we both agreed on what we wanted, it was just a matter of shopping for the right items and putting in a lot of work."

"You do have good taste."

"Thanks." She smiled. "The house is a lot bigger than it looks. Why don't you treat yourself to an unguided tour while I put on some clothes?"

"Don't go to any trouble on my account." He grinned, letting his eyes roam hotly over her. "Why don't you just take your coat off and relax?"

"That would destroy the mystery," she replied pertly. "And you know what they say. Reality can never match the fantasy."

"I'll take the chance."

She chuckled softly and shook her head. "I don't want

to ruin what might turn out to be a good working relationship." She hoped her message was clear. No matter how tempting it was, she couldn't allow anything further to develop between them. After all, he was her boss.

"You never know," he teased. "A little spice might improve our dispositions."

"What's this? Is the beast of sexual harassment rearing its ugly head?" She stepped into the bedroom, closing the door enough to obscure her from view, but not enough to impede their conversation.

He heaved an exaggerated sigh. "My sincere and abject apologies. Actually, I should look at this whole thing as a valuable learning experience."

"What do you mean?" she asked, searching frantically for clean clothes. Swearing that she'd never let the laundry get out of hand again, she rummaged through the closet and finally found a pair of well-worn but carefully mended brown slacks and an emerald-green sweater that matched her eyes. She dressed quickly.

"I've never had an accident-prone partner before."

"A couple of mishaps don't make me accident-prone. Besides, you said it could have happened to anyone." She stepped out of the bedroom.

He gave her a quick but thorough appraisal. "You look terrific."

"Thanks." Pleasure washed over her, but almost immediately it was replaced by embarrassment. Why was she so relieved that he still found her attractive? She tugged nervously at her sweater, readjusting it around her hips. Realizing that she had inadvertently drawn his eyes to the lower half of her body, Cassie tried to think of something to say to ease the growing tension between them. But her mind was completely blank.

"We should be getting back," Paul reminded her gently.

Feeling like a fool, she led the way outside. "What's on the agenda for this afternoon?" she asked, attempting to keep her voice light.

"Nothing earth-shattering. A few animals need vaccinations. Later, you can fill out some reports while I check on the camels. That's about it."

She nodded, locking the door behind her and following him to the car. As they began the trip back, she lapsed into an uneasy silence.

"What's on your mind?" he finally asked.

"I was just thinking of something you said yesterday. You mentioned being concerned about whether or not I could successfully handle this job, remember?"

"Yes, and I explained why."

"I was wondering if it goes beyond that." She looked at him. "Would you have been more comfortable working with a man?"

He thought for a moment, then admitted matter-of-factly, "Yes, I would have been able to deal with another man a lot easier than I can with a woman."

"I don't understand why."

His eyes were soft and warm. "I think you're going to bring problems into my life, Cassie. Problems I thought I'd never have to deal with again."

Suddenly she was nervous about the direction their conversation was taking. "If you mean my job performance..."

"That's hardly what I mean, and you know it." There was something infinitely tantalizing about his tone.

She had to stop this discussion before it went any further. "You're my boss, Paul, and I have no intention of allowing a personal relationship to develop between us. I like my job already, and the best way for me to keep it is to make sure my professional and private lives stay separate. Besides," she added, feeling desperate, "I don't want to hurt your feelings, but the truth is, you're not my type at all."

"That's not true, Cassie," he said softly, with a certainty she couldn't deny and a tenderness that melted her insides. He turned up the zoo's driveway and parked in his reserved space. "You're as attracted to me as I am to you. That's what's going to make our working together so interesting. I like being around you, and despite your protestations, I know when a woman finds me appealing."

All at once his arrogance infuriated her. "Oh, you do, do you? You conceited, self-centered egotist! For your information, I'm hardly even aware of you as a man!"

He regarded her for a minute, then burst out laughing. "Oh, sure. To you I'm just chopped liver, right?"

"Try stuffed turkey!" She stepped out of his car and slammed the door shut. With quick, angry strides, she crossed the parking lot and entered the lobby of the administration building. As she approached the doors leading to the clinic, she heard someone calling her name. She stopped and turned.

Debbie Stewart, the woman in charge of public relations, approached. "I heard what happened when you were treating the zebra, Cassie," she said, "Mac's been telling everyone how dedicated you are." She laughed. "What did Paul have to say about it?"

Cassie tried to mask her anger. "It doesn't matter. I'd be sincerely surprised if anything or anyone could impress a man who's as preoccupied with himself as Paul Kelly is." Her harsh tone surprised even her. Disgusted with the unprofessional way she had allowed her feelings to show, she shook her head. "Forget it, Debbie. I didn't mean that the way it sounded. Let's just say that Paul and I have a few problems we need to work out."

Debbie sighed. "He's been giving you a hard time." It was a statement that left little room for denial.

"You could say we have our differences."

Debbie nodded. "Why don't you let me buy you a cup of coffee. I think it's time we had a little talk."

Cassie was eager to accept. "You've got a deal, but first let me check to make sure Paul won't need me."

"I'll call from my office and tell him we've got to get some information from you for our records. It'll be all right. I promise."

Debbie's office was quiet and dignified, with wood-paneled walls and plush carpeting. In contrast to the starkness of the hospital area, it was filled with all the extras that turned a functional work space into a comfortable one.

Leading the way inside, she gestured toward a chair and poured two mugs of coffee. She handed one to Cassie, then sat down on the edge of her desk. "What I'm about to tell you is strictly off the record, okay?"

"Sure."

Debbie sighed. "I don't blame you for thinking badly of Paul, but there's a reason why he's being difficult. My husband and I were friends of Paul and Ruth for many years.

"His late wife?"

Debbie nodded. "She died about two years ago. Paul was devastated. He threw himself into his work, which helped him get over the worst of it, but he hasn't been the same since. By now I had hoped he would have started dating, but he refuses to see women socially. He's a very attractive man and, believe me, he's had lots of volunteers, but his pattern is always the same. He shows no interest in anyone, particularly the persistent ladies.

When he encounters a woman he really does like, someone he feels he could become serious about, he either
avoids her like the plague or does something to deliberately alienate her."

"Just what are you trying to tell me?"

"All I'm saying is that until now he's successfully
dodged situations that might endanger his solitary lifestyle." She smiled. "But now you've come along. He
has to deal with you every day and, to make matters
worse, it turns out you're not only beautiful, you're also
single!"

"And because he doesn't feel he's completely in control of the situation, this makes him very uncomfortable?"

"Exactly."

"I think I understand," Cassie said thoughtfully. As
she mulled the idea over in her mind, her anger toward
Paul vanished. She turned to Debbie. "I'm not sure how
to handle this, but I can't thank you enough for telling
me. Now that I know, it'll be a lot easier for me. I owe
you a great deal."

"Wait until you get your first paycheck. Then you can
buy me an expensive lunch!"

"You've got it!" Cassie laughed. "I'd better be getting
back to work now."

"If you need someone to talk to . . ." Debbie's tone
assured Cassie that the invitation was genuine.

"Thanks." As their eyes met, Cassie felt certain she'd
found a friend.

CHAPTER
Four

As she entered the hospital wing a short time later, Cassie could hear Paul saying, "Just set the crate down over there. I'll take care of it as soon as I finish with Horace."

Passing one of the curators in the hall, she entered the examination room. The area was filled with polished stainless-steel tables, sterile packs, and numerous instruments duplicated in an assortment of sizes. Electrocardiogram and anesthesia equipment lined one wall. She was vaguely aware of the familiar odor of disinfectant.

Paul was busy with a young chimpanzee. He glanced up and scowled at her. "It's about time. For a while I thought you and Debbie had decided to abscond with hospital funds and fly to Mexico."

Cassie checked the wall clock and grimaced. "I'm terribly sorry. I had no idea we had taken so long." Feeling guilty for leaving him shorthanded she offered eagerly, "Would you like me to take over?"

He laughed. "I realize your intentions are good, but you're not exactly experienced yet. We have quite a variety of animals here. It will take you some time to learn to recognize and treat them all."

"Oh, come on." Again he was questioning her ability, and she was still determined to prove her worth. "I may not be an experienced zoo vet, but I do have many years of schooling. A primate, whether it's a baboon or an orangutan, is still a primate. Our dosages are gauged on weight and species, so there's no problem unless you think I'm not knowledgeable enough to differentiate between an elephant in the *Proboscidea* order and a squirrel, who belongs with the *Rodentia.*"

He shrugged casually, as if the matter no longer merited discussion, but there was a mischievous gleam in his eyes as he said, "Fine. While I put Horace back in his crate, why don't you take Jack over there?" He gestured toward the far side of the room, where one of the keepers was crouched next to the wall, peering into a crate.

As Cassie's eyes came to rest on his name tag, the elderly man's face turned bright red. "Not me, ma'am. He means little Jack." He pointed inside the wire cage.

Cassie laughed. "Don't worry, I wasn't about to attack you, syringe in hand."

The keeper brought out a creature the size of a small house cat. The furry animal had enormous bright orange eyes. "This is Jack, ma'am." The man regarded the animal fondly. "Be good now, boy."

Cassie stared uncertainly at the animal. What in the world was it? She glanced quickly at Paul and caught the smug look on his face. She'd been set up. Well, she wouldn't give him the satisfaction of letting him win this round.

She studied the animal carefully. It was obviously a civet, and it looked very familiar, but there were so many species, and so many common names to remember. Its spotted leopardlike coat was dense, almost velvety in appearance. That was her best bet in identifying it. If she kept her wits about her, maybe the name would come to her.

"It's the fur, you see," the keeper explained. "Those bald patches he's got all over are really beginning to worry me."

"I can see why." Cassie bit her lower lip thoughtfully, feeling Paul's eyes on her. "These animals are so valuable." She stroked its fur. "It's not often I see one of these."

Instead of the response she had hoped for, something along the lines of "Whatchamacallits are really not so rare," or "Diddlypoos are almost extinct," the keeper simply nodded and said, "Jack's a bit of a rascal, but he's my favorite."

As she stroked its fur, the animal reared its head and nipped her hand between the thumb and forefinger. With a yelp, she jumped back.

"Doc, I'm sorry! Did he get you?" The keeper pushed the animal down onto the table, holding it still. "I thought I had him. I really did!"

"It's okay." She smiled reassuringly, though her hand

throbbed painfully. "He didn't even draw blood. I expect he was just trying to tell me to speed up the examination."

"Let's see." Paul came over and inspected the bite.

Cassie pulled back her hand. "I'm fine, really." She didn't want him to think she couldn't handle herself around exotics.

"If you'd like, I can finish the examination for you," Paul offered.

"Thank you, but I'll manage."

She sensed his struggle to keep a straight face. "Whatever you say." Leaning against the counter, he crossed his arms in front of him and watched her.

Cassie washed her hands at the sink, fighting an urge to throw the bar of disinfectant soap at him. His superior attitude was making her angrier by the minute. Trying to look composed, she returned to the animal's side. But one look at her grim features made Paul chuckle out loud. Trying to cover it with a cough, he left the room, thus giving her a chance to continue the examination in peace.

Adjusting the overhead light, she tried to get a better look at the diseased areas. The patches weren't bald, as she had initially thought. Instead, the hair seemed to have broken off, leaving only stubble behind. At the center of each patch was a reddish area. Cassie picked up a small light fixture and plugged it in.

"Do you need more light, Doc?" the keeper asked. "Maybe I can move back a little."

She shook her head. "This is a Wood's light. If those patches show a distinctive greenish glow under it, then I'll know what's bothering our little friend." Shining it on his coat, she watched as the areas turned a deep lime color. "Just what I thought," she said.

"Is it serious?"

"No. Jack's going to need treatment, though. It looks like he has ringworm." She began clipping the hair away from each infected area. "I'm going to place some salve on the patches, and then I want you to take him to the quarantine area. In the meantime, keep an eye on any of the animals he's come into contact with. Ringworm is infectious."

"How long before I can take him back to his pen?"

"I'll check again in a week and let you know." She washed her hands again. "Make sure you wash your hands, too," she warned him. "Ringworm quite happily attacks humans."

He nodded. "I remember now. Our dog had it once. We put some ointment on, and it just went away."

"Like I said, it's nothing serious, just a fungus infection."

"Thanks, Doc."

"Anytime." She watched as the keeper placed Jack back into his crate and carried it out, talking softly to the animal, all the while. Cassie smiled, feeling satisfied with her work.

Just then, Paul stepped through the doorway. "How's the hand?"

"Fine." With a great show of energy, she began putting her instruments away.

"You did a good job." She started to smile, but paused as he added, "Considering you had no idea what you were treating."

She stopped in mid-motion. "What?"

"I saw the look on your face. You forgot the name. For future reference, Jack is a linsang."

Cassie finished putting the instruments into the autoclave for sterilization. "Didn't your mother ever tell you nobody likes a smart aleck?" she asked, trying to keep a straight face. "I knew it was a civet; I just couldn't recall the common name for that particular genus."

"Okay, I'll let you off the hook this time," he replied with a wink. "Besides, I've got a date with a camel in less than five minutes."

She smiled. "There's just no accounting for taste. Want me to come along?"

"No. I want you to make a full report on the linsang. Take any one of our patient files to use as a model. Then go into the cabinet, pull the patient's record, and add your report to it. After you're finished, have it all on top of my desk."

She nodded. "Anything else?"

"If you find yourself with nothing to do, go to the mammal nursery. Our spider monkey is having a problem with the milk formula. He's drinking more than enough, but he's still losing weight, so it looks like we're going to have to enrich it. See what you can do."

"Fine."

"I'll meet you back here as soon as I'm through," Paul said on his way out of the clinic.

Cassie listened as his footsteps echoed down the hall. She hated paperwork, but it was an inescapable part of her job. Reluctantly, she returned to Paul's office and cleared off the small table he used as extra counter space. She placed the chair reserved for visitors in front of it. From now on this would be her desk.

Next she gathered the materials she needed from the records room and made out a detailed report on the linsang's condition. But she was dissatisfied with the way it read and rewrote it several times before finally placing the folder on Paul's desk and heading for the mammal nursery.

A young redheaded technician glanced up as she entered the room. "Hi, I'm Sally James. I'm in charge of this area. Is there something I can help you with?"

"I'm Dr. Prentiss."

The young woman smiled warmly. "I heard we had a new doctor on our staff. I'm so glad to meet you. Tell me, how do you like working here?"

"I like it a lot." Cassie waited for Sally to finish feeding a lion cub. "I hear you've been having a problem with the spider monkey's formula."

Sally nodded. "The baby should be putting on weight, but he isn't. In fact, although I've increased the amount he's getting, he's still hungry at the end of each feeding and he's actually losing weight."

Cassie nodded. "I'll need to see his chart."

Sally placed the cub back in its crate and led the way to an incubator. "Here you are. Both patient and record."

Cassie watched the young animal. It did look frail. She studied its medical history, and then, realizing she needed additional data, she pursed her lips thoughtfully. "Sally, I'll have to do some research on this formula before altering it. I'd like to take this chart with me, but I'll bring it right back, okay?"

"Sure."

Cassie spent the next hour looking through all of Paul's research books. She wasn't sure which ingredients to increase and which to maintain at the same level. Paul was bound to return soon, and she was so anxious to please him that she gathered her courage and called the local university. The research lab there raised baby monkeys. Perhaps they'd know what to do.

Her gambit worked. After a brief conversation she knew that adding ten percent more evaporated milk would give the mixture the necessary richness. She returned to the nursery and handed Sally the chart, explaining the change.

She was feeling good when she returned to her office and found Paul sitting behind his desk. "How did it go?" he asked.

Cassie filled him in while he studied her report. His silence unnerved her. Scarcely breathing, her heart pounding, she waited, praying he'd approve.

Five minutes later he glanced up. "This report is excellent, Cassie. And that was good work on the formula. You're coming along just fine." He glanced at her makeshift desk. "I'm also glad to see how resourceful you can be."

His praise thrilled her, and she grinned broadly. "Thanks."

He retrieved their coats from the hook on the back of the door. "Here you go. It's time to call it a day."

Cassie accompanied him to the parking lot, stopping by her car to wish him good night. As she placed her keys in the lock, he said, "I got an estimate on the repair bill for my car earlier this afternoon. We're going to have to get together and work out a way for you to pay for the damages."

Her heart sank. So much for her good mood. "You're right. It's time to get that settled so we can put it behind us."

"Good. Why don't we meet for dinner at around seven."

She hesitated. She mustn't allow the evening to turn into a date. "I can't. I have to pick up some jumpsuits at the store. It's about time I looked like the rest of the staff. Afterward, I want to go home and get those patches sewn on. I probably won't be through until after eight o'clock. Why don't we make it around nine?"

"I'm expecting a call at that time." He paused. "I'll tell you what. Why don't you come over to my place. We'll have a drink and work out the details."

So much for keeping it impersonal. Again she hesitated, but then decided that this just might work to her advantage after all. It was a work night, so if she didn't arrive until nine, she'd have a perfect excuse to leave after an hour or so. In the comfort and privacy of his own home, Paul might become easier to negotiate with, and she needed the advantage. It was absolutely imperative that she convince him to accept a schedule of payments low enough to suit her tight budget.

"Fine," she replied. "I'll see you then."

CHAPTER
Five

IT WAS EXACTLY 9:00 P.M. when Cassie arrived at Paul's house. As she stood on the porch waiting for him to answer the door, she marveled at the sprawling ranch-style mansion. Even in the darkness it was easy to tell that this was no ordinary house. The massive, intricately carved wooden doors had probably cost as much as all her furniture put together.

Paul greeted her warmly. He was dressed in well-worn jeans and a turtleneck sweater that clung to his lean frame, emphasizing its muscular contours. With a sweeping wave of his hand, he gestured her inside. "You're right on time. May I take your coat?"

Suddenly the high-voltage force of his virility engulfed her, clouding her senses. To her embarrassment, it took her several long seconds to understand what he'd said. Reacting at last, she slipped her arms out of her coat.

She watched him as he carried it to the hall closet, appraising him openly as he stood with his back to her. His sweater stretched snugly over his broad shoulders, accentuating their powerful width. The tight jeans, slung low on his slim hips, encased nicely rounded . . . Her skin prickled with an unexpected rush of heat. Guilt and desire mingled, leaving her in a state of excited confusion.

Paul turned, watched her for a moment, and then graced her with an appreciative grin. His blue eyes were mesmerizing in the muted light. Quickly averting her gaze, Cassie looked down. His sleeves were pushed up, revealing strong, masculine forearms.

With some effort, she shifted her attention to her surroundings. From the foyer she could see a plush sofa in the living room. A Persian rug, woven in tones of red and blue, covered the floor. The draperies had an expensive custom-made look. "You have a lovely home," she said.

"Thanks." He led her down the hall to the den and proceeded to the bar in the corner of the room. After opening a bag of pretzels and a large can of peanuts, he began searching through the cabinets. "There's a bowl around here somewhere," he muttered. He declined her offer to help. "Look around. Make yourself at home," he suggested.

She began a leisurely exploration. Oaken bookcases, filled with a variety of hardcover and paperback volumes, stood against the far wall. A coarsely woven wool rug with a geometric design set off the seating area. On it lay a massive old dog of indeterminate origin.

With a gasp of delight she approached the gray-brown creature, who gazed at her silently out of tired brown eyes, his tail wagging slowly. The dog was so ugly that Cassie decided he was cute. She bent down cautiously.

"He won't bite," Paul said. "As a matter of fact, he's very friendly once you get to know him. His name is Burglar."

"How in the world did he get that name?" she asked, scratching the big dog behind his floppy ears.

"About three years ago we discovered that some animal was digging and tunneling through the zoo's south fence at night. Each morning the groundskeeper would find the trash can near the concession stand upturned and its contents littered all over the place. We tried to catch the culprit several times, but he always eluded us. Finally, one evening when I was working late, I discovered Burglar. We got to be real good friends, and we've been together ever since."

Touched by Paul's story, Cassie glanced down at the scruffy mutt. Burglar had fallen asleep.

A loud snap from a log burning in the fireplace diverted her attention. She studied the art objects on the stone mantel. Two brass planters with rosewood stands stood on either side of an Early American antique clock.

"What will you have to drink?" Paul asked.

"Madeira, if you have it."

"I do," he said, pouring her some.

As she picked up her glass, Paul motioned her toward the couch. Stretching out his legs, he placed his feet on the coffee table and leaned back. "Now, how do you propose we settle this mess with my car?"

Considering his luxurious lifestyle, she found his preoccupation with quick payment annoying. "Where's your estimate?" she said tersely.

He fished a piece of paper from his pocket. "This is the best price I found."

Her eyes widened slightly at the sum. "You're sure this is right? I thought it would be much higher."

"That's what they quoted me."

Feeling immensely relieved, she let out a long breath. "I was prepared to ask you to let me pay you back in installments, but this isn't nearly as much as I expected it to be." She mulled the figure over in her mind. "I think I'll just make out a check for the entire amount right now. That way we can forget about it."

"Are you sure? You can pay me back a little at a time, if it makes things easier. I don't want to put you in a bind."

"Thanks for offering, but I'd rather get this squared away now." She signed the check and handed it to him. "When will your car be fixed?"

"The shop said I could drop it off before work tomorrow. They'll give me a ride to and from the zoo, and by the time I'm ready to go home, it should be ready."

"Not bad." She stood up, feeling suddenly uncomfortable to be sitting so close to him on the couch. "Now that that's settled, I think I'd better go home."

"Before you go"—he stood facing her—"I want to apologize for being so rude to you before. I had no right to speak to you that way."

She hesitated, not wanting to divulge anything Debbie had told her, but wanting to let him know she understood. "Don't worry about it. We all say things we don't mean."

"Please, sit down and let me explain." His voice was

husky, soft, and irresistible. Her knees felt weak.

"There's no need. It's over and done with."

"Please."

Before she knew it, she was sitting next to him again. An inexplicable panic spread through her. She didn't want him to explain. The last thing she needed was to sympathize with him. She felt vulnerable enough already.

"Cassie," he said gently, holding her gaze with his own, "you're the first woman I've been seriously attracted to since Ruth died. And, I sensed you were also attracted to me." When she started to protest, he held up a hand. "Please let me finish." She lapsed into an uneasy silence.

"When I realized what was happening, I wanted to put as much distance between us as possible. That's why I said those things to you. I thought if I could make you dislike me, you'd quit and I'd never see you again." He paused. "Then, when you left my car, I realized what I'd been doing. I've been trying to hide for too long, Cassie. You see, to me starting a relationship means taking a risk I don't want to take again. So instead I've isolated myself and have been living a very empty life."

"Paul." Her voice wavered. "I'd like to be honest with you. You're my boss, and I don't want to get emotionally involved with you. Yes, I do think you're a very appealing man. But can't we just enjoy the attraction, that special chemistry between us, without doing anything about it?"

"Is that what you really want?" He regarded her intently.

She fought the desire to nestle against his chest and feel the warmth of his embrace. "That's just the way it's got to be," she replied, avoiding his question.

"I won't pressure you." He tilted her chin with his forefinger. "The result will be the same, you know. Certain things are impossible to fight."

She swallowed. "Please don't say that!" As she reached for her purse, her hand trembled slightly.

"I've upset you, and I'm sorry. But I've gotten into the habit of saying exactly what I mean." He gave her a sheepish smile. "As you can well imagine, that's not always a good thing." He shifted closer to her. "If you stay and keep me company a little while longer, I promise not to say anything else that will make you angry."

Cassie hesitated. Something told her she should head for the door as quickly as her feet would take her. But much to her surprise, she remained seated. As she looked up at him, she saw herself reflected in his dark blue eyes. For a moment she was pulled downward into a deep well of sensuous, primitive desires. Breaking the spell, she jumped up from the sofa. Obviously he was fully aware of his effect on her.

She made a great show of studying the titles in the bookcase. A snapshot in a corner caught her eye. Against a majestic backdrop of snowcapped mountains, Paul stood with his arm around the most beautiful woman Cassie had ever seen. The woman's brilliant smile seemed to add a sparkle to the glittering snow, and her long, blond hair shone in the sunlight. "What an absolutely breathtaking woman!" Cassie exclaimed.

"That was my wife, Ruth." Paul's voice was unemotional, almost cold.

Cassie's heart twisted. Of course it was Ruth. "She's exquisite," she said softly.

"Ruth was an incredible woman. But she's part of my past." Paul's words were measured, his tone carefully controlled, almost as if he were speaking about a casual acquaintance.

Suspecting that beneath the calm surface lay turbulent emotions, Cassie immediately regretted having brought up the subject. Quickly, she placed the photograph back on the shelf. "I'm sorry. I didn't mean to bring back any painful memories."

His fingers wrapped tightly around his glass, his knuckles turning white with strain. Afraid it would shatter in his hand, Cassie opened her mouth to speak but stopped as he finished his drink in one gulp and set the glass aside. "It isn't painful anymore," he said. "I've accepted her death. That part of my life is over."

Despite his disclaimer, she sensed his profound sense of loss and her heart ached for him. She was desperate to change the subject. "This house is so . . ." She fumbled for the right word. "So perfect. I really envy you," she exclaimed, rejoining him on the couch.

"You'll have to come back during the day. The grounds are extensive. The only drawback is that there's a lot of work involved with the upkeep and maintenance." Smiling, he shrugged. "Then again, I wouldn't have it any other way. If I lived in the city where I couldn't have land around me, I'd die of claustrophobia."

"I understand exactly what you mean. I don't like city life, either, but I also don't want to be too far from one."

He laughed. "Yes, I know. You want pastoral seclusion without having to give up the benefits of the city. My thoughts precisely."

As Cassie finished her drink, he brought a large decanter over to the coffee table and refilled her glass. She sipped it automatically. "You know, the only thing I regret is that I didn't have the cash to buy a house with more land around it. At the prices they were asking, all I could afford was a quarter of an acre. But your place is gigantic. How many acres did you say you have?"

He chuckled. "You're not at all subtle, are you? I can almost hear the questions racing around in your mind."

"Not really," she replied in a disinterested tone. "I have it all figured out. You're really a hit man for the mob."

Paul laughed. "Not quite. The fact is, I just got lucky. I stumbled onto this place quite by accident. I wanted a home, and one of Ruth's friends told us about John Ryan, the former owner. He had just been transferred abroad and he needed to sell fast. He was even willing to accept a rental agreement. We snapped it up right away. It was the best deal I've ever closed in my life. About a year later he decided he didn't want to bother with it anymore and offered to let me buy it at a ridiculously low price. I took it immediately. I'd be willing to bet that my payments on this place are lower than yours."

"If I'm starting to turn green, don't mind me."

He chuckled. "That's all right. Green's a good color for you. It matches your beautiful eyes." He walked to the bar and poured himself another scotch.

The unexpected compliment caught her by surprise. Unable to think of a reply, she simply smiled. He returned to the couch, sitting down much closer to her. Warning bells went off in her head.

"Something bothers me, Cassie," he said in a seductive voice.

"What?" She sipped her drink casually, trying desperately to hide her uneasiness.

"You're afraid of me."

"No, I'm not." The denial was automatic. She gave

him what she hoped was a confident smile.

"If I get too close to you, you start twirling your hair."

She hadn't realized what she'd been doing. Dropping her hand to her lap, she shrugged. "It's a habit."

He placed his hand over hers. "I want us to at least be friends. But we can't be that if you're not comfortable around me."

She pulled her hand out from under his with the pretext of having to brush back her hair.

"Every time I touch you, you look as if you're ready to crawl out of your skin."

"You're imagining things."

His hand enveloped hers again. "Am I?"

This time she didn't move. His touch heated her blood, warming her to the very core. Her eyes met his, and he smiled.

"Cassie, the fact that we work together shouldn't keep us from becoming friends."

She nodded. Her heart was pounding so loudly she was surprised he couldn't hear it. "I agree." She glanced at her watch. "Speaking of work, I think I'd better be getting home."

"Do you have to?"

She nodded and rose.

In the entryway he helped her slip on her coat. "I'm glad you came tonight, Cassie."

"So am I."

As she stood there, tying her belt, Paul reached around her to open the door. She turned to wish him good night, but the sound of squeaking hinges made her spin abruptly, then reel backward as the edge of the door struck her squarely on the forehead. Pain shot through her, and she staggered.

Paul caught her before she fell and supported her until she had regained her balance. "Cassie! Are you all right?"

"I . . . I'm not sure." Dazed, she touched her forehead gingerly. "Ouch!"

Muttering a curse, Paul kicked the door shut and lifted her into his arms, forestalling her protests with, "Don't try to talk."

"But I'm fine." She struggled, trying to disengage herself. "Please put me down."

"Cassie, shut up and enjoy the ride." His arms tightened around her as he headed down the hall to the den.

Something told her it wouldn't do any good to argue. She relaxed in his arms, breathing in the lemony after shave that mingled with his male scent. His heartbeat was strong under her ear. Her steely resolve melted against the warmth of his body.

Paul strode across the room and set her gently on the couch. "Now let me take a look," he ordered gently.

"I'm fine," she insisted, although her temples throbbed with a powerful headache. Automatically she reached up and felt carefully. "No blood. That's a good sign," she said with forced cheerfulness.

Reaching across her, Paul switched on an antique brass lamp. He adjusted the shade and inspected her forehead. "You'll live," he declared laconically, but his expression remained fierce.

"Whoopee," she said dully. "I don't suppose you have a gallon or two of aspirin you could spare."

He laughed. "Sure. You can have a handful before you leave. On second thought, I'll be chivalrous. Leave a handful and take the bottle."

"Thanks." She sat up slowly. "I really don't know what's come over me lately. I'm usually not so clumsy." She paused, then added with false brightness, "Now I know I'm faced with a man who'll stop at nothing to sweep me off my feet."

Scowling, he ignored her dig. "That bump looks nasty. Lie back down, and I'll get an ice pack."

"Never mind. I'll just go home and..." She stood, wobbled, and dropped back onto the sofa. She shook her head in dismay, and the throbbing pain made her stomach lurch. "Oh, my!"

Paul pushed her gently back onto the pillows. "Lie still," he insisted. "Are you feeling faint?"

She tried to sound confident and healthy. "No, it's just one of those dizzy spells everyone has when they get up too fast. The only ailment I've got is a splitting headache." She squinted, trying to shield her eyes from the lamp's bright light.

Immediately Paul reached over and switched it off. Their bodies seemed dangerously close in the intimate darkness. The dying fire illuminated the room with a flickering glow that cast long shadows on the wall.

Paul didn't move back. Leaning over her, he whispered, "Feeling better?" His hands gently brushed a strand of ebony hair from her face. "This light suits you, Cassie."

Her thoughts reeled as she struggled to keep her emotions in check. The bump on her head seemed to have muddled her senses. He was so close and so tempting! His bronzed skin gleamed in the firelight, urging her to touch him, to feel the strength and gentleness that made him so thoroughly a man. Her respiration quickened perceptibly, and she struggled to catch her breath. As his eyes lingered on her lips and moved down to her breasts, her whole body turned liquid with longing. She could barely think, couldn't speak, as she tried to grasp the frail ropes of a quickly fading reality.

His palm stroked her cheek then moved lower, caressing her throat and neck. "Don't be afraid, Cassie," he whispered, his voice soothing her, lulling her into a dream.

She couldn't tear her eyes away from his. As if enchanted, she couldn't stop the waves of desire that washed over her and left her trembling. "I don't want—"

He placed his fingers on her lips. "I won't let anything happen, Cassie. Trust me."

She was being foolish, yet a need more powerful than any she had ever known held her motionless before him. A shiver of delight ran up her spine as she felt his warm body against hers. She was throbbingly aware of his every movement as he traced an imaginary line from her cheek down to her neck.

Through clouded eyes she saw his mouth part slightly as his lips moved to capture hers. "Cassie. Such a lovely name for an equally lovely woman." He murmured the words over her lips before closing the gap between them.

At first his kiss was gentle; then slowly it deepened and intensified, to a mind-searing onslaught that left her giddy and deliciously weak.

Slipping a hand down her arm, he laced his fingers with hers. "How I wish you were mine for the taking." His eyes were burning with hungry need and a barely held restraint.

She reached out to him and her hand encircled his neck, pulling him gently toward her. He needed little inducement. In an instant his mouth had covered hers again. Their lips clung for a sweet eternity, exploring the moist, yielding surfaces. Their tongues clashed with fierce urgency.

Finally, with a groan, Paul pulled away from her. "I promised I wouldn't let anything happen tonight, but I'm only human. I'd better take you home, or you'll end up making a liar out of me."

Cassie's throat felt so tight she could barely swallow. She trembled with the effort to dispel the heated tension pulsing inside her. Breathing deeply, she tried to calm her racing heart. "I don't understand what's happening to me."

He smiled gently. Standing, he offered her his hand and helped her up. "It's very simple, Cassie. We're falling in love."

His bluntness surprised her. "No, I can't...I mean, I don't want to."

He sighed. "What we may or may not want isn't going to play a big part in any of this, I'm afraid." He brushed a swift kiss across her lips. "Don't worry, Cassie. I'll never betray your trust in me."

As they walked down the hall she wrapped her coat tightly around herself. Only one thought burned in her mind—she had to escape. She had to get away from his house as quickly as possible. More than anything, she needed the safety and sanity of her own home. "I'd better go. My car is just outside, so don't worry about giving me a ride. I'll be fine."

"Cassie, you're not fine." He reached for her arm. "Wait a minute. I never even got to fix an ice pack for your head."

"I'll get one at home." She disengaged herself. "I'll be there in less than ten minutes. Believe me, I'm perfectly all right."

He sighed. "Call me the second you arrive?"

"Sure." Not wanting to give him an opportunity to argue further, she strode toward the door.

"Don't forget." He held the door open for her.

"I won't." with a casual wave, she left.

Darkness encased her on the drive home. Her knuckles tightened around the wheel as she tried to sort out her feelings. How could she have let things get so out of hand? Paul was her boss!

As she recalled his kisses, her pulse quickened and a warm glow enveloped her. Even Craig had never made her feel that way. She trembled slightly. Paul had said they were falling in love. Did that mean he felt the same way? Had it been special for him too? Of course not! She answered her own question almost instantly. What was she thinking? Kissing her had only been his way of apologizing for knocking her on the head, although the whole clumsy incident had been her fault.

If she had any doubt about her importance to him, all she had to do was remember the look in his eyes and the tone of his voice when he'd spoken of Ruth. Despite his disclaimer, he still had strong feelings for her. As Debbie had pointed out, Paul's love for Ruth had been too deep to end with her death. The woman who succeeded Ruth in Paul's affections would have to live with the knowledge that she was second best. And that fact, Cassie thought, tolled the final requiem for whatever might have been between them.

CHAPTER
Six

CASSIE CONSIDERED CALLING in sick the next morning. She simply couldn't face Paul. She had acted like a fool the night before. What ever had possessed her? There seemed to be a certain magic in the air whenever she was with him. She had felt it from the very start.

Knowing more about Ruth, and Paul's recent loneliness, made her even more susceptible to him. She felt an almost instinctive need to reach out and comfort him. Terrified by her own emotions, she resolved to erect a barrier around herself, a wall that would keep her safe and protected. Her involvement with Craig had taught her a lesson. Paul Kelly was a v   poor risk. Keeping that thought in mind, she drove to the zoo and entered their office.

The idea of sharing such confined quarters with Paul bothered her a great deal. Being around him was like playing with nitroglycerin—one wrong move and she'd go up in smoke. There was no escaping it: the more contact she had with him, the harder it would be to keep her mind strictly on business.

She smiled as a new thought occured to her. Perhaps now that she was wearing the jumpsuit used by the staff, she'd find it easier to maintain a professional relationship with Paul. It was certainly bound to dispel his romantic ideas. She looked about as sexy as a sack of potatoes.

She glanced up nervously as Paul entered the office. His shiny brown hair tumbled over one eyebrow, giving him an appealing little-boy look. He smiled "Good morning. How's your head?"

"Just fine," she said, giving him an impersonal smile. "Where do you want me to start this morning?"

Paul adopted an equally no-nonsense tone. "Check the nursery while I take care of all the hospital patients. After that we'll meet back here and make rounds. Mac should be bringing us the 'sick reports' any time now."

Cassie kept her eyes on her desk, avoiding even a casual glance in Paul's direction. Maybe if she didn't look at him, the attraction between them would fade. She cringed inwardly. Logic like that was bound to get her nowhere.

Feeling painfully self-conscious, she walked across the room to the coffee maker and began preparing a fresh batch. "Want some?" she asked.

"Sure would."

She could feel Paul's eyes on her, but rather than acknowledge them, she feigned great concentration on the task of measuring the proper amount of grounds into the filter. "It'll be ready in a minute."

"No rush."

"Is there anything you can do about getting me a regular desk?"

"You'll have one before long, I promise." He cleared his throat. "I know things are hard enough for you, particularly now that you feel so awkward around me."

Cassie's heart pounded. Trying to mask her reaction, she strolled casually back to her seat. "You're imagining things."

Paul smiled knowingly. "Whatever you say."

Ignoring his comment, she picked up her medical bag and walked to the door. "I'm going to the nursery."

Paul followed. "Wait a minute, will you!"

She stopped abruptly. "Yes?"

"I thought you said we could still be friends."

"We are."

"Don't look now, Pinocchio, but I think your nose is growing."

Cassie flushed with embarrassment. "Do you want to stand here all day, or do you want to get some work done?"

Paul sighed. "What I really want is to ask you to have dinner with me tonight. I'd like to sweep you off your feet and dazzle you with my spectacular company." He grinned engagingly. "And if you say yes, I'll even promise not to make a pass at you."

"Paul, we're just asking for trouble." She felt thoroughly exasperated with herself and wished she had kept her mouth shut. It was one thing for Paul to think she didn't trust him, but now she was afraid he'd realized that she didn't trust herself around him either. "What I meant to say," she corrected herself quickly, "was that if we spend all day working together and go out then socially in the evenings, we're going to end up hating each other within a week."

He gave her a mocking smile. "Not likely."

The blood was pumping so loudly in her ears that she barely heard herself answer. "Excuse me, Doctor, but I'd better get going."

"Running away won't help, you know." His eyes sparkled with a roguish gleam, and she had the distinct impression he knew precisely how she felt, how her hands were sweating and her heart was pounding. She was furious with him, but most of all she was furious with herself for not being able to stop the sudden rush of confusion every time he came near her.

"I realize you find yourself utterly charming," she said sarcastically, "but I'm afraid my estimation of you doesn't quite match your own. Now will you please get out of my way?"

He continued to block her path. "You're cute when you're angry," he teased.

She groaned. "That's an old line."

"I was desperate."

There was something infinitely contagious about his smile. Laughing, she shook her head. "I give up! If you want to stand here all day, it's fine with me."

"Say you'll have dinner with me," he insisted softly.

She shook her head. "Sorry. I hardly ever do anything under coercion."

"Hardly ever? Aha! So there's hope after all!" She started to walk around him, but he stopped her with a hand on her shoulder. "One last chance? Remember, men like me don't grow on trees!"

"No, they swing from them!" she shot back good-naturedly and ducked quickly past him.

"Wait!"

She stopped. "What now?"

"Before you go to the nursery, give me a hand in the examining room, will you?"

"Sure." She sighed, certain he'd taken her refusal to go out with him as a minor, temporary setback. The good doctor was not about to be dissuaded. The thought made her nervous. She would have to find a way to discourage him once and for all. Paul Kelly was definitely hazardous to her mental and physical health.

She followed him down the hall. As they entered the clinic, she spotted an oddly shaped crate on top of a metal table. "What's that?" she asked, frowning.

"It's a boa someone donated to the zoo. It's supposed to be tame, but be careful with it. Usually I'd have the reptile curator here while we examine it, but since he's out sick and the keepers are busy moving one of the alligators to a new enclosure, it looks like we're going to have to rely on each other."

"I can handle it by myself," Cassie retorted matter-of-factly. "Why don't you look in on some of our other patients?"

For a moment Paul just stared at her, and then he said, "I can't tell you how tempted I am to let you go it alone. It might teach you a lesson. Unfortunately, if you become instant snake chow, all hell is going to break loose and I can't afford to let that happen."

His sharp words made her realize that, by implying she could handle the snake alone, she had inadvertently belittled his safety precautions and indirectly questioned his own abilities. Her lack of tact was uncanny. Chiding herself for speaking without thinking, and realizing that he was very angry, she bit her lower lip and tried to think of a way to mend matters. Then again, maybe it was just as well. If he stayed angry with her, she could keep him at bay without much effort.

"It's an ugly-looking snake," she commented absently as she peered inside the crate.

"Didn't anyone ever tell you that some of the finest things in life look repulsive at first?" Paul's playful tone surprised her.

Cassie chuckled. So much for his staying angry. Despite her effort to remain aloof, relief washed over her. "In that case, take heart. There's hope for you after all," she said.

She opened the crate door and waited a few moments. Paul darted a quick glance in her direction. "Be careful. It's supposed to be a pet, but you never know; and with a boa you want to avoid getting bitten at all costs. Even though they don't usually strike, those sharp little teeth can inflict one heck of a wound."

"I'll be careful." Beginning to show signs of life, the animal started slithering out. Cassie grasped it behind the head with one hand and draped its long body behind her neck and around her shoulders. The creature began to undulate and wrap itself around her. Gently, it circled her waist and ribs and even tried to crawl beneath her lab coat.

Cassie studied the snake for any signs of illness. Everything seemed normal. It's skin showed a healthy fluorescent gleam as the light caught the rippling green scales. It's body looked strong and agile.

"Will you be careful?" Paul faced her, drying his hands on a towel. "That thing is all muscle. If it coils, you're in big trouble."

"He's just playing," Cassie said. Taking the ophthalmoscope from the counter, she held the snake's head and examined its eyes. It clung to her more tightly.

"Don't let it do that!" Grasping the creature firmly, Paul stopped it from coiling further.

The snake pulled against his grip and suddenly contracted its muscles. Bracing himself, Paul held his ground, but the motion tossed Cassie off balance. The ophthalmoscope flew out of her hand and she crashed against Paul. Winding tightly, the snake crushed them together.

Paul muttered an oath. "Now you've done it!"

"You made it angry," she accused, keeping a firm hold on the snake's head.

"Made it angry? I was trying to help you out." Struggling with the snake's long body, Paul shifted his grip to the animal's midsection, inadvertently brushing Cassie's breasts. Instinctively, she drew back.

"I'm trying to keep us from getting crushed to death, and you're worried I might make a pass at you?" He was furious.

Cassie twisted sideways, struggling to increase the gap between them. "I've got to get some working room."

Paul groaned as she hit him below the belt. "Watch your elbow! I'm fragile in spots, too, you know."

She flushed with embarrassment. "Sorry. But if we don't start working together, they're going to have to scoop us out of these coils with a spatula."

"Actually, maybe we should just relax. I'm starting to enjoy this." He pressed closer against her and nuzzled the side of her neck.

"Paul, stop that! This is hardly the time or place." But her pulse skyrocketed, and her head seemed light enough to float away.

Paul chuckled. "Cassie, don't fight it. Something more powerful than you or I is drawing us together." He dove for her lips, but she eluded him and stepped on his toes.

"Ugh!" He hopped around on one foot, threatening to

throw them both off balance. "Ah, my sweet, you have a sharp tongue but an even sharper heel." He eyed the boa's fangs warily. "And that snake has an even sharper bite. Enough fooling around. Help me uncoil it, starting with the tail."

"It's about time you decided to cooperate," she said drily.

Five minutes later they stood facing each other, flushed and gasping for breath. Triumphantly, they held the snake outstretched between them.

"Let's get it on the table," Paul ordered.

Running his hand over the smooth scales, he examined the boa for any unusual growths below the skin. Satisfying himself with its external appearance, he took the head from Cassie's hand, pried open the jaws, and checked the interior of its mouth with a pen light. Cassie noticed that the membranes were moist and showed a healthy pink color.

"Everything looks in order," Paul said. "I think we can keep it. Let's send it to the reptile house. It'll probably need feeding right away."

They both looked up as the mammal curator entered. "Hello, Mac. Something we can do for you?" Paul asked.

"I just wanted to tell you I left the sick reports on your desk."

"Okay. We'll get to those in a little bit. In the meantime, is there any chance we might talk you into taking our newest resident to its keepers?"

Mac regarded the snake distastefully. "If you put it back into its crate, I'll take it away."

Paul and Cassie each held an end and gently placed the boa back in its crate. "Here you go, Mac. Thanks."

"Dont't mention it."

As Mac's footsteps faded down the hall, Paul riveted

Cassie with his eyes and walked toward her, stopping so close that she could feel his warm breath on her cheek. "Cassie, you owe me something."

It was impossible to resist the spell his nearness cast over her. Her knees trembled as she tried to pretend he was having absolutely no effect on her. "I don't know what you're talking about."

"Admit it. You enjoyed wrestling with me and the snake." His eyes held a mischievous twinkle. "And you owe me the kiss you so effectively avoided."

"Don't be ridiculous," she scoffed, then gasped as he closed the space between them and took her into his arms.

"Do you have any idea what you're doing to me? I used to be an even-tempered guy, with an uncomplicated life . . ."

"Long time ago, in a galaxy far, far away." She pulled away from him and leaned against the counter, trying to strike a casual pose. He gave her a look that said he saw through her pretended indifference.

"Cassie, you're amazing." He shook his head and gazed at her tenderly. "My practice was relatively unexciting until you arrived. You seem to have a distinct knack for attracting the bizarre."

She meant to tell him it wasn't true, that she didn't attract the bizarre. It was just that she'd been having a bout of rotten luck lately. She couldn't explain it; but ever since she'd met him, things had been going wrong. She meant to tell him all this, but his eyes held her mesmerizingly, and to her utter dismay she realized she couldn't speak.

Just then one of the curators came running in. "Doc, we have a problem. Two of our rhinos have started fighting again."

Immediately the spell was broken. Suddenly all business again, Paul picked up his medical bag and dashed out the door. Cassie stood immobilized, unable to decide what to do. Paul ducked his head back. "Get moving, will you!"

She nodded, lunged for her bag, and ran after him. Catching up with him by the ambulance, she climbed into the passenger's seat and held on while he criss-crossed the park, speeding down empty paths and across back access areas.

The rhino exhibit was less than two minutes away from the hospital, yet by the time they arrived the two large males had already inflicted serious injuries on each other. One lay on its belly, refusing to rest on its side and admit defeat, while its companion stood over it, looking slightly dazed. Their gray, dust-covered hides were covered with severe, penetrating wounds that would require immediate medical attention.

"This happens from time to time with our males," Paul explained as they left the vehicle and approached the back gate. "The problem is we just don't have the facilities to keep them separated."

Taking a CO_2 gun from his bag, he loaded it with a heavy dose of tranquilizer and instructed Cassie to do the same with hers. "You aim at the one on the ground. I'll take the other. They'll both have to be completely under before we can approach safely."

Both darts hit their mark. Cassie waited beside Paul and the keepers while the sedative took effect. The large, victorious rhino strutted nervously around the enclosure before finally coming to a halt. As if watching a film in slow motion, they saw the one-and-a-half-ton animal fall to his knees and then topple onto his side. His less for-tunate sparring partner had already succumbed to the powerful drug and lay in a similar position, resting peacefully.

Paul nudged Cassie forward. "Let's go."

They traversed the exhibit area and knelt beside the animals, then began to pour disinfectant over the injured areas. Using special needles, they closed the gaping wounds.

"Now what?" Cassie asked. "As soon as they come to, you know we're going to be treated to a repeat performance."

"We'll have to keep one of them in the holding pen behind the exhibit."

"It's not fair to confine a healthy animal indefinitely," she protested.

"We don't have a choice."

"We could remove their horns," she suggested.

"No way. The dirt they use to protect their hides would produce an infection, no matter what we did to prevent it. We'd be forced to confine them for months."

"So what's the answer? Imprison one of the animals, but rotate them periodically so they both get equal time in jail?"

"Something like that," he admitted as he began putting his supplies away. "Until we can find another zoo willing to take one of them, there's no other solution. But if you want to take one home for a few days, be my guest."

"Very funny."

By the time they reached the gates, the keepers were driving one of the still-groggy rhinos into the holding pen. "They'll be all right now," Paul said quietly.

"I suppose so."

"Let's leave the ambulance here and take a walk around the park. It's good practice to visit each of the enclosures as often as possible. If you're on friendly terms with your patients, it's usually easier to enter their pens to administer some disagreeable treatment when necessary."

She smiled. "Is that theory like the chicken-soup one— it may not help, but it can't hurt?"

He chuckled and for a brief moment she felt very close to him. "I guess so. What do you say? How about that walk?"

"Sounds good to me."

Side by side, they strolled down the access alley moving from one enclosure to the other. Paul stopped frequently to say a few words to each of the animals. To the ones who readily approached the back gate, he gave a scratch behind the ear or a gentle pat on the head.

He introduced Cassie to his favorites, the sure-footed llamas and two members of the wolf pack he had raised from cubs. His comments, sometimes laced with the medical jargon they both knew so well, revealed the special fondness he felt for each of his charges. His easy conversation made Cassie feel an accepted part of his world, no longer an outsider.

For the first time she sensed a special relationship evolving between them. They shared so much! She felt comfortable with him. She enjoyed his company. It was that simple, yet that complicated.

As they passed the gazelles' exhibit, Paul stopped. "You know what? This could have been a very boring day, but you've made it interesting." His eyes held hers as his lips curved into a smile. "Cassie, I really *would* like us to be friends. It's been a long time since anyone really made me laugh." His voice, tempered with sorrow, was gentle.

The sadness in it rippled powerfully through her. She wanted to help him, to comfort him. No! What was she

doing? Panic welled up inside her. She must not allow
him to touch her emotionally. Her only hope lay in turning the conversation to a lighter vein. "You're either
being very insulting or very charming, and for the life
of me I can't tell which," she said.

"I'm being truthful." He looked at her as if seeking
her understanding. "What do you say? Can we really be
friends?"

Their gazes locked. Cassie's heart raced as she struggled for something to say. She felt trapped, caught between the voice of sanity, which urged her not to give
in to his charms, and a deeper need that compelled her
to take the chance.

As she contemplated turning away, her throat constricted and her stomach plummeted. She knew then that
her decicion had already been made. No matter how hard
she raced, she'd never outdistance the fear she was so
afraid to face. Perhaps it was time to stop trying.

"Yes, Paul," she affirmed in a whisper. "I'd like very
much to be friends."

CHAPTER
Seven

CASSIE SAT BACK in her chair and smiled. Today marked the end of her third week of employment at the zoo. Things had started to settle into a comfortable routine. She and Paul had remained friends, and fron his actions she'd concluded that he, too, realized the danger of mixing their professional and personal lives. He seemed to be making an effort to limit their contact to the office. In fact, since the day they had agreed to be friends, he hadn't telephoned her at home or encouraged any type of socializing beyond an occasional lunch to discuss hospital business. It was a good arrangement . . . or at least a safe one.

After glancing at her watch, Cassie gathered her papers and stacked them neatly on the side of the table. It was time to go home. She was about to turn off the lights when Paul strode into the room. "I'm glad I caught up with you."

She was instantly alert. "Is something wrong?"

"No, nothing like that. I just haven't seen you all afternoon, and there's something I wanted to ask you."

"I'm listening."

"The Forest Service is giving a lecture this evening at the university. They're going to start trapping and tagging some of the wild javelinas that inhabit the southwestern part of the state. A national foundation wants to study their behavior. Since I'm hoping to convince the Forest Service to donate a few of these animals to our zoo, I thought we could go tonight and see what their program involves."

"Sounds interesting."

"Afterward we can discuss it. Maybe we'll learn something that will be useful in terms of our practice here at the zoo."

"Fine. What time does it start?"

"Eight o'clock."

"No problem. Shall I meet you there?"

"It doesn't make sense to take two cars. You're on the way for me, so why don't I pick you up after dinner, say around seven-thirty?"

From his tone she concluded that, once again, this was to be strictly business. She felt a twinge of disappointment, then chided herself for being a twit. After all, wasn't this what she'd wanted? "I'll be ready," she assured him.

As she walked to her car, Cassie fought an overwhelming sense of regret. She felt as if a heavy burden were resting on her shoulders. She had wanted a nice business relationship with Paul, and now she had it. Why, then, did part of her yearn to make it more than that?

Cassie stood in front of the mirror carefully scrutinizing her appearance. Wanting to look different tonight, she had let her black hair fall in smooth waves around her shoulders, and her green eyes were accentuated by the dark green Oxford-style shirt she wore tucked neatly into a pair of snug black slacks.

The doorbell sounded, and she went to answer it. "Hello, Paul. You're right on time. Would you like to come in and have something to drink before we go?"

He shook his head. "We don't have time."

"In that case"—she grabbed her purse—"I'm ready to go."

She felt unaccountably nervous as she slipped into the passenger's side of his sports car. The leather interior was plush and comfortable, yet her stomach was tied into so many knots she could scarcely enjoy it.

Paul was polite but aloof as he drove into the city. They chatted about inconsequential matters, but to Cassie it seemed his mind was miles away.

"Paul," she said at length, "have I done something to make you angry?"

He looked at her in surprise. "Of course not. What made you ask that?"

"You're acting strangely, that's all."

He smiled. "It's nothing. I've just got a personal problem I have to work out."

"Can I help?"

He shook his head. "It's not something anyone else can help me with." He shrugged. "It's just one of those things I have to think through."

She nodded slowly. "I understand."

"Good. Then you can start heaping sympathy on me. I love to be pampered when I'm feeling sorry for myself."

She laughed. "Poor baby!" she said, and patted the back of his hand.

"Ahhh!" He gave a satisfied sigh. "Much better!"

As he turned into the university parking lot, he gestured ahead. "That's where it's going to be held. I hope we can find a parking space close by." It soon became obvious that they'd be lucky to find any spot inside campus, let alone near the auditorium. "I'm going to drop you off at the door. That way you can save seats for us while I go find somewhere to park."

"No problem."

Cassie found the auditorium almost empty. The small crowd of twenty seemed dwarfed by their surroundings.

A tall, very thin man in his early fifties stood at one end of the room, glancing nervously at the papers in his hand. The dark green U.S. Forest Service uniform confirmed his identity. Sensing he was not used to speaking in public, Cassie walked up to him and introduced herself. Maybe what he needed was a friendly face to help put him at ease.

"Hi, I'm Dr. Cassie Prentiss. I work at the Albuquerque City Zoo. You must be Dr. Mike Sanderson."

"It's a pleasure to meet you, Dr. Prentiss." He shook her hand.

She smiled warmly. "Just call me Cassie."

"If you'll call me Mike." Something in his smile and energetic manner suggested he had an enormous zest for life.

"Mike it is then." She sensed his interest in her and

was flattered by it. "It's starting to fill up," she said. "I guess you're going to have quite a few students at your lecture tonight."

"I don't know which is worse, having the auditorium almost empty or having it full."

Cassie laughed. "Why do I get the impression you're not used to giving these presentations?"

"Possibly the fact that I'm about to have a coronary tipped you off."

She smiled sympathetically. "If it's any consolation, the few minutes before a speech are the hardest. Once you begin talking, it'll be a snap."

He smiled sheepishly. "I'm in charge of field operations, not public relations. It's just that no one else knew much about this project."

"So you were elected?"

"Precisely." Just then Paul joined them.

Cassie introduced the two men. "Mike's the vet in charge of the Forest Service's field operations," she explained.

"Oh, I'm not a vet," he corrected. "I've got a doctorate in vertebrate zoology."

"Oh, I'm sorry. I just assumed . . ."

"It's okay. Most people assume the same thing you did. Usually I don't correct them. It just leads to more questions, like 'What is a vertebrate?'"

Paul laughed. "In that case, I think I'd handle it as you do."

Mike glanced at his watch. "I'd better start my lecture. It's been a pleasure meeting you both. By the way, if you'd like, I'd be glad to keep you posted on our progress. We're always glad to cooperate with the zoo if there's anything we can do to help."

"We'd appreciate that, Dr. Sanderson," Paul replied, shaking his hand.

"See you later, Cassie." He beamed her a smile.

"'Bye, Mike."

The minute he was out of earshot, Paul gave her a sharp look. "So it's Mike is it? That was fast work."

"Mike is his first name. I thought I said that when I introduced you." She hadn't failed to recognize the slight edge in his tone, but she wasn't about to acknowledge it.

"That's not what I meant."

"Then what did you mean?"

He glowered at her.

Not waiting for his reply, she followed the crowd down the aisle. "We'd better hurry or we won't get a seat near the front."

The minute the lecture ended, Paul stood up to leave. A full moon illuminated the sidewalk, as they crossed the almost deserted campus. Paul remained silent, and the shrill cry of a night bird echoed in the stillness. Cassie shivered in the evening breeze.

"Here." Paul took off his dark blue windbreaker and placed it over her shoulders. The jacket was still warm from his body. His arm encircled her protectively, pulling her closer as they walked.

Acutely conscious of his nearness, Cassie tried to subdue the frantic beat of her heart. Inhaling the heady, masculine scent of his cologne, she wondered what it would be like to melt into his arms. A need rose inside her, filling her, urging her to take a chance. Still, she fought it, struggling against her desire.

Suddenly, Paul stopped in mid-stride and muttered an oath.

"What's wrong?" Following his angry gaze, she saw

that his car had a very flat left rear tire. "I hope you have a spare," she said.

"Of course I do, but I can't imagine what happened." He stooped down next to the flat. "I guess I must have picked up a nail or something."

"Can I help?"

"Sure. You can change the tire while I watch."

"And deprive you of the opportunity to dazzle me with your strength and skill?" She feigned shock. "I wouldn't dream of it!"

"Heck, I just wanted to give *you* the opportunity to show me how liberated you really are." He went to the trunk and took the spare tire from the well. "How about looking for something to block the front wheel so the car won't roll when I jack it up?"

"That I can do. Being the totally feminine and charming creature that I am," she teased, "I'm perfectly content to take the subordinate role."

"You'd make that supreme sacrifice as long as it helped *your man,* right?"

"Of course," she replied. Then, as she realized what that implied, she felt her face burn. "I mean—"

"Too late." He flashed her a smug grin.

Cassie watched as he tapped off the hubcap and tried to loosen the lug nuts. He cursed softly. "I can't budge these."

"Want me to try?" she offered.

"No. I want you to go to the trunk and get me my oil can."

"Right." She found it after a brief search and tested the squeeze handle carefully. The spout was clogged. "Hey, this thing doesn't work."

"Of course it works. Just aim it at the nut, will you?"

Cassie started to protest, then decided to give the can

a good shake before trying again. Standing close to Paul, she shook the can and watched a lock of brown hair fall over his eye as he struggled to loosen the nut. His arm tightened as his muscles strained, and her blood surged in response. All at once she felt an overwhelming desire to touch him. Then, suddenly, the top of the oil can flew off. Oil spurted from the container, splattering over the side of Paul's shirt and down his right pants leg.

He leapt to his feet. "I don't believe you! I said to aim it at the lug nuts, not me!"

"I'm sorry! It wasn't coming out of the spout, so I thought I'd shake it and . . ." Her voice trailed off as she watched the dark oil seep through his clothing in ever-expanding circles.

Grimacing, he pulled the soggy material away from his body. "I should have remembered you were accident-prone!"

"It wasn't my fault. You didn't tighten the lid!"

"Oh, Lord! Even my underwear is soaked!"

"There's some oil still left in the can," she ventured hesitantly. "Want me to pour it over the bolts?"

"Nuts."

"You can do it yourself if you want to." She held out the oil can.

"I was speaking literally: these are nuts, not bolts." He shook his head and grabbed the can from her hands. "On second thought, you're right. I'd rather do it myself."

Feeling miserable, Cassie watched in silence while he finished changing the tire. For what seemed like the hundredth time, she wondered what was wrong with her. Ever since meeting Paul she'd been so distracted and clumsy that terrible things kept happening. She was beginning to think she was as dangerous to him as he was to her!

Lost in thought, she conjured up a mélange of satisfying scenarios: saving Paul from a charging camel; rescuing him from a coiling boa; and changing all four tires in record time.

"All right. It's done," Paul finally announced.

Still in a world of her own, Cassie smiled dreamily. "It was nothing."

"Nothing to you maybe, but my shorts feel slimey and soggy. If you don't mind, I'd like to change before I drop you off."

She gasped, realizing what she had said. "I'm sorry. I didn't mean that it was nothing...I was just thinking of something else." She shook her head. "I mean—"

He groaned with exasperation. "Will you get inside the car?"

She practically dove in. As they headed toward his home, she searched frantically for something to say, but once again words failed her. She stared out the window, thoroughly dispirited.

"Don't worry about what happened," he said gently after they'd been driving for a few minutes. "It's just been one of those days. Everyone has them—although you can't deny that lately you've had more than your fair share."

She smiled ruefully. "That's a polite way of saying I seem to be acting the role of Typhoid Mary, or Accident Mary, as the case might be."

"Maybe you've been sent to Earth to dispense retribution. In which case, I must have done something very bad to deserve all this punishment."

She grimaced. "And maybe the bird singing outside

your window tomorrow morning will be a buzzard."

"I think that already happened this morning."

Their eyes met, and they laughed.

"Well, at least it wasn't a boring evening," Cassie said at last.

"Life's far from dull when you're around." A tender smile touched the corners of his mouth.

Trying to keep the conversation from assuming a more intimate tone, she said, "You must admit I've improved at work."

"Yes, I was beginning to miss the little catastrophies that seemed to follow in your wake."

"See how lucky you are? Now you see that I haven't lost my touch."

When they arrived at his house, they were both still in good spirits. As Paul opened his front door, Burglar came bounding up to them. Paul stooped to pet him. "Hello, boy."

Cassie watched silently. For a moment she wondered what it would be like to become part of Paul's family. A warm feeling spread through her at the thought. But when Paul turned to look at her, she averted her eyes quickly, afraid he'd somehow read her thoughts.

"I'm going to go change," he said. "Will you take Burglar out to the backyard for a little walk?"

"Sure." She called the dog to her and patted his head. "How do I get there?"

"Just go through the den and into the kitchen. The door is on the far left. You can't miss it. Go outside, boy," he ordered. As Burglar took off, he added, "Follow him. He knows the way."

Cassie laughed. "Okay."

The moment she opened the door leading to the yard, Burglar dashed outside. Wrapping Paul's parka around her, Cassie followed. Moonlight filtered through the elms in silver beams that danced upon the dark ground. Branches rustled pleasantly in a gentle breeze.

Stopping by the base of a brooding pine, she turned and glanced back at the house. A bright light caught her attention and she found herself staring through a partially opened curtain right into Paul's bedroom. Shielded by the darkness outside, she stood and watched as he stripped off his shirt, revealing a powerful, hair-darkened chest. He unbuckled his belt and tossed it on the bed in one careless motion, then unzipped his pants. She watched transfixed as he dropped them and removed his underclothes.

She inhaled sharply at the sight of the most spectacular male body she had ever seen. The blood ran hot in her veins. Her breath quickened as she studied him, memorizing every detail. How she yearned to explore that body through touch as she was now discovering it through sight!

Cassie gasped as she felt something cold and wet against her palm. She looked down to see Burglar nudging her. Bending, she scratched the animal behind the ears. "Oh, Burglar," she whispered tremulously, "how I wish I could make love with your master."

"Cassie . . ."

She jumped up and spun around. Paul stood before her, naked to the waist, tight, low-slung jeans covering his lower body.

She swallowed. "Paul!"

His eyes burned into hers. "If you want something, Cassie, you must reach out and take it. Don't ever be afraid to tell me what you want." Slowly, as if in a dream, he drew her into his arms and smothered her faint protests with a fiery kiss that sent her senses reeling. Her mouth parted under the tender onslaught of his tongue, inviting him to deepen his fevered exploration. Moaning, she pressed herself against him, molding her soft contours to his hard body, feeling the swell of his rising passion pressing against her with intoxicating promise. Resistance melted and something primitive stirred to life at the very center of her being. She clung to him desperately, feverish with unresolved longing, seeking the comfort of his touch and the sweetness of his caress.

In one fluid motion he lifted her off her feet and into his arms, then carried her effortlessly back into the house. He entered his bedroom and placed her gently on the bed. A single lamp at the corner of his dresser gave off a muted light that made his skin glow. His muscular forearms tensed as she ran her fingers lightly over them.

"Make love with me, Cassie," he pleaded. "It's what we've both wanted from the very beginning." He stepped out of his jeans and stood before her, beautiful and relaxed. He held out his hand to her, and she accepted it. Her heart pounded in her ears as she waited, quivering in anticipation.

He stood so close that she could feel the heat radiating from his body. His hands were steady as he undressed her slowly, his fingers caressing her skin with fleeting promise, awakening fires deep inside her. She met his heavy-lidded gaze as he pulled her into his arms, and she thrilled to the feel of his naked body against hers. For a moment he simply cradled her, seemingly content to have her near him. Gradually she began to sense the hunger in him, the incredible need that drove them both to seek what only the other could provide.

At last Paul stepped toward the bed and guided her down beside him. His lips met hers, tasting, exploring with languorous passion that left her feeling thoroughly desired. His hand slid from her waist to seek the soft fullness of her breast.

"You feel so good," he murmured.

"Paul." Her body arched toward him of its own accord. Her lips sought his throat, then moved over his shoulders nipping gently, teasing him, tormenting him into a frenzy of desire. She buried her finger in the rough, curly hair that covered his chest, delighting in the masculine feel of him.

He gave a low, throaty groan as her hands slid ever downward. Exhilarated by the power of her own femininity, she reveled in the pleasure she could bring him.

She turned her mouth toward his in silent invitation. He didn't hesitate. His tongue surged hungrily between her parted lips, reaching into her very soul. Open to his love, she melted against him, wanting him to fill her, to make her whole.

"Oh, my sweet, beautiful Cassie." His lips sought the tips of a breast and he teased it with his warm moist tongue.

No part of her escaped the caresses that seared her flesh. Her body seemed to erupt in flames, tortured by the skill of his expert lovemaking. His words soothed her when she thought she'd die of wanting, then brought her to the edge with sensuous promises.

Acknowledging her surrender, he covered her body with his own. "I love you, Cassie. I've loved you for a long time."

They melted together. He moved in powerfully descending strokes that consumed her with blazing passion. She gave herself up completely to the moment, not thinking, only feeling the wondrous burst of sensation that coursed through her. With one final cry, their spirits fused, soaring toward heaven and floating suspended among radiant stars.

Paul shifted to his side, taking her with him and holding her close to his heart. He stroked her hair. "I'll never let you leave me, Cassie."

His words conveyed a grief that she knew came from the past, and her heart cried out to him. "I'll never leave you, Paul." She pushed slightly away from him until their eyes met. "Don't you know? I love you, darling."

He buried his face in her neck, holding her so tightly that she gasped for breath.

"Help!" she cried, laughing, her voice muffled in his powerful chest.

He eased his hold on her and chuckled. "I'm sorry. Am I keeping you from something important, like breathing?"

She smiled and rested her head in the crook of his arm. "Who needs to breathe anyway?"

"I never thought I'd be this happy again," he whispered.

"I'm happy, too."

"Our lovemaking is so right. It's just the way it should be, my pretty lady, free-spirited, with no reservations or restrictions."

A sense of deep contentment filled her. Whatever doubts still plagued her, she would not consider them now. Resting in the haven of Paul's arms, she drifted off to sleep.

A short time later, or so it seemed to her, Cassie opened her eyes. A beam of light played on the far wall. Puzzled, she glanced at the clock on the nightstand. It was almost six in the morning!

Judging by his even breathing, Paul was still asleep. Cassie crept silently into the bathroom, emerging minutes later wrapped in one of Paul's robes, her teeth and face scrubbed, her hair brushed.

She woke him with a kiss. "Good morning."

He opened his eyes. "Is it time to get up already?"

"Uh-huh." She studied his sleep-relaxed features. A day's growth of beard covered his face, yet instead of looking scruffy, he looked sensual. She basked in the warm intimacy of waking up with the man she loved.

Reluctantly she remembered that it was a work day. "You've got to get dressed and drive me home so I can shower and change," she told him gently.

"What time is it?"

"Six-thirty."

"We've got time. We don't have to be at work until nine."

"I know, but I have a few errands to run this morning."

He stretched lazily. "All right. Hand me my pants."

She shook her head and, with an impish grin, bolted from the bed, taking his pants with her to a chair across the room. She leaned back comfortably. "Get them yourself."

"Wanton woman." Chuckling softly, he tossed the covers aside and walked naked to the closet. He returned her lingering gaze. "Lucky for you I'm not modest."

"Would you deny me this simple pleasure after all we've been through?" she teased.

"Who's denying you?"

She surveyed him thoroughly. "I'm glad you're not one of those people who believe that lechery should be confined to the male of the species."

He laughed. "I'm all for equal rights. You have every right to be as lecherous as I intend to be." His eyes narrowed, and he gave her a wicked smile. "Remember that."

"Uh-oh. That sounds ominous."

"Now be a nice lady and go feed Burglar. His food is in the pantry. One cup mixed with water will do."

She stood and saluted. "Yes, sir!"

He slapped her on the bottom as she scurried away. After feeding Burglar, Cassie poured herself a glass of juice. It was going to be a beautiful day! She felt languorous and content as she sipped the frosty liquid. She was in love with Paul. Why had she fought her feelings for so long? She shook her head. It all seemed so silly now. Paul wasn't a bit like Craig. She had nothing to fear. Even working with him would not be difficult. It was just a matter of maintaining a professional attitude on the job. Their personal lives need not interfere.

A loud noise in the den brought her to the doorway. Paul was cursing as he picked up the fallen contents of his desk. She started to step forward to help when she saw him freeze. A snapshot had fallen out of one of the books. Even from where she stood, she could see that it was a picture of him and Ruth.

His expression changed. Standing up slowly, he stared at the photo for long moments, his features contorted with sorrow. Suddenly he jammed it back between the pages of the book and tossed it angrily on top of his desk.

Cassie's throat constricted and her thoughts whirled. What did his expression mean? Was he still in love with Ruth, still mourning her death? Suddenly all his words of love, all his tender caresses, were thrown into doubt. How could he love her, Cassie, when his feelings for Ruth were obviously still so strong?

Slipping back into the kitchen, Cassie decided to pretend she hadn't seen anything. It wouldn't do either of them any good to argue over what couldn't be changed.

CHAPTER
Eight

THE BUBBLE HAD BURST. Cassie felt a dull heaviness inside her as they drove to work. It numbed her senses and left her feeling curiously detached from reality. Perhaps, if she could maintain that feeling, nothing could touch her again. Or hurt her. She stole a glance at Paul. His eyes remained on the road.

"We've still got plenty of time, and I don't mind making a few stops before going to work," he said. "Would you like me to wait for you while you get dressed?"

Was there a peculiar undercurrent to his tone, or was it simply her imagination? She couldn't tell. "No, I'd rather take my own car. I have some errands to run this afternoon, too."

"I don't have any plans. I'll be glad to drive you wherever you have to go," he offered.

"No, thank you." At once she realized how cold her words sounded. She'd given herself away. He was bound to ask questions that she didn't want to answer.

He regarded her quizzically. "Is something wrong?"

"No," she lied, hoping to avoid any further discussion.

"You're worried about work, aren't you?" He pursed his lips. "If it's any consolation, I've been giving that a lot of thought too. Teaming up to treat patients, seeing each other constantly, and trying to maintain a professional attitude is going to be difficult. Particularly because I'm still your boss."

"No need to worry on that score," she said. "I don't expect any special treatment. I'm still a professional, Paul; you won't have to remind me to behave like one at work." Her voice sounded strained.

He frowned. "Why are you acting so aloof all of a sudden? What's going on?"

As he pulled into her driveway, she sighed with relief. "I'm not being aloof," she said, stepping out of his car. "Thanks for the ride back."

"Cassie, wait!"

She kept walking, "I can't. I don't want to be late for work. I'll see you later."

The moment she stepped inside her house, she took a deep breath and tried to organize her thoughts. There was no escaping the fact that she had made a mistake by falling in love with Paul Kelly. This time, however, there would be no running away. She needed her job too badly. She'd have to shut him out of her thoughts and look to the future without even a casual glance backwards.

By the time she was ready to leave for work, Cassie had convinced herself that if she could fall in love with Paul, then she could also fall out of love with him. There was little sense in loving a man who could not return her feelings in full measure. Now she knew that Ruth would always stand between them. And if she couldn't have all of Paul's affection, she didn't want any of it.

She tried to fight the bitterness welling up inside her, but she couldn't help feeling betrayed. In her mind's eye she could still see the pained expression on Paul's face as he beheld Ruth's picture. There had been a hopelessness to it, a raw quality that had touched her deeply, chilling her to the bone. Was she overreacting now out of a fear of being rejected once again? She discarded the idea.

As her thoughts wandered, she recalled Paul mentioning a problem he was struggling to deal with, something she couldn't help him with, a very personal matter that only he could work out. Had he been talking about his memories of Ruth? And if he had, could that mean she, Cassie, had only been a substitute all along, someone to help ease the pain of losing the one woman he truly desired? She gasped as the full impact of that possibility struck her.

Picking up her purse, she walked down the hall. She had another hour before she had to be at work, but she had no intention of sitting around moping. She'd put the time to good use by stopping at the cleaners and the drugstore. She was about to close the front door when Paul drove up. Frozen to the spot, she stared as he strode toward her. Something in the set of his shoulders warned her that he intended to force a confrontation.

"All right, let's have it." He grasped her arm and led her back inside. Slamming the door behind him, he faced her squarely. "What's gotten into you this morning?"

"I don't know what you're talking about." Her voice was flat and emotionless.

"Stop, damn it! Don't insult my intelligence. Something's wrong. Now let's hear it!"

"What do you think it is?" she challenged with a stony glare.

"I honestly don't know, although you obviously think I should. As far as I know, I haven't done anything to anger you. You were fine this morning, and then all of a sudden—"

"This conversation is pointless," she interrupted, "and I really must take care of some things." She started toward the door, but he reached out and grabbed her arm.

"We're going to talk, so you might as well lead the way back to the living room and pick a comfortable place to sit down. Unless you'd rather discuss it right here in the hall."

"I don't have to put up with this. I'm leaving." She shook free of his grasp.

"No, you're not." He towered over her.

She stood her ground, though it was difficult to think as the heat of his body seared through her clothing, warming her skin like a caress.

"Look at you!" he exclaimed. "You're trembling! You're in love with me, yet you insist on shutting me out." He shook his head in bewilderment. "No more games, Cassie. We both deserve better than this."

She wanted to open up to him, to share her fear of losing his love to Ruth, of competing with a memory. But she couldn't, not now. She was sure he would say that Ruth belonged to his past and that she, Cassie, was the only one who mattered to him. Perhaps he even believed it himself. But she knew better. She had seen his face, devastated by the photo and scarred by memories. To him, Ruth was as alive as she'd ever been.

Instead, Cassie told him only part of the truth. "Paul, I still hurt from the last man I loved and lost. I just can't go through that again."

"Cassie, You must know I would never do anything to hurt you."

Stepping away from him, she tried to gather her courage. "Once before, I thought I was in love. Craig wanted an open and carefree type of relationship. I couldn't handle it, because to me love implies commitment. It means giving and sharing all of myself, allowing another person to see everything that makes me who I am." She stopped, afraid that if she continued she'd lose the tenuous grip she had on her emotions. "Craig couldn't give me what I needed. He wasn't ready for that type of relationship. Now I'm not sure I'm ready."

"If you truly love me, how can you walk away?"

She bit her lip. She couldn't let him know that Ruth was the reason she wasn't ready—and might never be. He wouldn't understand. She tried to convey with a look the feelings she couldn't put into words. "I need time, Paul. Will you give me that?"

Their gazes held; then he turned restlessly and ran his hand through his hair. At last he nodded. "I'll give you time. I can be patient as long as I know we have a chance."

Two weeks passed. True to his word, Paul stopped pressuring her. But even though she pretended not to notice, Cassie was aware of the way his eyes followed her whenever they were together. She wanted to reach out to him, to tell him how much she missed being with him, yet fear kept her silent time and time again. How could their love hold the magic for him that it did for her, when he would always be measuring it against a memory?

Should she trust him enough to allow her heart free rein? She longed to believe in his love, but what would happen to her years from now if she woke one day to find she'd been right all along and Paul never truly had belonged to her? The pain of knowing she had lived a lie would be unbearable; she knew it would destroy her.

After finishing with her last patient for the day, Cassie returned to their office. Bone-weary, she slumped unceremoniously into her chair. As she leaned back and stretched, Paul walked in.

"I should have never come to work this morning," he said.

"What's wrong?"

Visibly startled, he turned to her. "Oh, I didn't even see you."

"Gee, thanks," she teased. "It's nice to be noticed."

He gave her a half-hearted smile.

"What's wrong?" she persisted.

"It's Edna, our largest African elephant. When Mac told me she wasn't acting right, I wasn't really worried. But I decided to check with Pete, her keeper. Last night he filled her water trough as usual and left her half a bale of hay, six loaves of bread, and a bucket of potatoes. This morning he discovered that she had scarcely eaten any of her food, yet she kept wanting more water. He filled the trough twice, and still she kept begging for more. That's when he realized that her skin was much hotter than usual. By the time I got to her enclosure, she was leaning against the wall for support."

"I've never seen an elephant lean against anything," Cassie said.

"My thoughts precisely. It was obvious that the animal was really sick. Her ears were folded back against her neck and shoulders, and her tail was hanging straight down instead of swishing back and forth. I ran my hand over her foreleg and along the back of her body. It felt as if I were rubbing hot cement. I knew I had to get an antibiotic into her, so I told Pete not to give her any more water. I thought I'd put the stuff in her water trough, and she'd drink it all down once she got thirsty enough."

"Did she?"

"No. I knew the medicine was going to taste bitter, so I made her wait all afternoon for a drink. I even had Pete take her out of the area while I filled the trough and mixed one-third of the powder in with the water. I figured I'd give it to her in three doses so it wouldn't taste quite as bad."

"What happened?"

"She drew up a couple of gallons with her trunk and started to eject it into her mouth. Then her expression changed, and she aimed her trunk at Pete and blew that medicated water all over him."

Cassie couldn't keep from smiling, though she knew the situation was serious. "Getting an injection through an elehant's thick hide is all but impossible," she said. "What are you going to do next?"

"I'm not sure, Cassie, but I've seen one other elephant with this type of infection before, and they go down pretty quickly. I'm going to have to find a way to get that antibiotic into her, and soon."

"Look, I don't have much experience with this type of animal, but I'd still like to take a look at her. Would you mind?"

"Not at all. Let's go."

As they crossed the park, Cassie falling into step beside him, he said, "I've missed you the past few weeks." His voice was soft and gentle.

Her heart twisted with pain. "I've missed you too, Paul."

"Cassie, I—"

"Don't say it. Please."

"Why won't you trust me?"

"Paul! I need time to sort things out. I've wanted to end the rift between us more than you can imagine, but I'm afraid. Before I do anything, I've got to make sure I'm doing the the right thing and for the right reasons."

"Cassie, if I could only make you listen to me!"

She shook her head. "I don't want to talk about it anymore. Let's concentrate on your patient."

They fell silent as Pete approached. "Have you come up with an idea, Doc?"

"Not yet." Paul glanced at Cassie. "Maybe Dr. Prentiss will be able to help."

Her thoughts drifted as she studied the four-ton animal before her. "Pete, does Edna like junk food? I'm thinking of something nice and sweet, like ice-cream cones."

The keeper nodded. "She loves them. Before we had the moated enclosures, she'd take as many as people would give her. She never got tired of them."

"That could be the answer," Cassie said, beaming. "We'll mix the antibiotic in a quart of ice cream and spoon it onto cones. We'll have a keeper she doesn't know feed them to her, and just to make sure she doesn't suspect anything we won't doctor the first few. If we pick something like caramel fudge, or another flavor that's especially sweet, we should be able to mask a lot of that bitterness."

"Doc, that's a terrific idea!" Pete's face lit up.

Paul looked pleased, too. "I knew you'd make a great

zoo vet, Cassie!" he said softly. Turning his attention to Pete, he began to question the keeper about Edna's habits. "Since you've already fed her, Pete, I think we'll wait until about eleven this evening. By that time she should be ready for a snack."

"But who's going to give her the cones, Doc? The staff will be long gone at that late hour."

Cassie didn't hesitate. "I will. She doesn't know me, so it should work out just fine."

Pete agreed. "I'll get the ice cream from the concession stand. They'll have a quart to spare, I'm sure. Shall I bring it to you at the hospital?"

"Yes," Paul replied slowly. "Cassie, just to be on the safe side, I think you'd better change into street clothes. That should set her even more at ease."

"Good thought." She paused. "We'll mix up Edna's snack and place it in the freezer. When we're finished, I'll go home, change, and have dinner. We can meet back here at around eleven."

As they returned to the hospital area, Paul said, "Look, I think it's silly for both of us to drive back here when you're on my way. Let me pick you up."

"I don't know..."

"Cassie, don't be so damn stubborn, for heaven's sake!"

"All right, all right. What time should I expect you?"

"I'll be at your house at ten minutes after ten."

They entered the building, and Paul held the door open for her. "You know, we do make a good veterinary team. Our ideas as well as our methods complement each other. Yours begin where mine leave off, and vice versa." Though his praise made her heart sing, she remained silent. "You're a good partner, and a very good vet, Cassie," he added.

She glanced at him, not sure how to respond.

"I mean it," he insisted. "I'll always be glad I hired you, even if I end up losing you in the way that's most important to me."

"Paul, I—"

"You don't have to say anything. Here comes Pete with the ice cream. Go home, Cassie. I'll see you later tonight."

There was a lump in her throat as she nodded. "See you then."

CHAPTER
Nine

CASSIE HEARD PAUL drive up just after ten. She was
unwilling to invite more problems by asking him in, so
she met him outside. Giving him no chance to get out
of the car, she opened the door on the passenger's side
and slipped inside.

He greeted her curtly.

Ignoring his tone, she tried to keep hers light. "I hope
you appreciate that I'm wearing my famous 'street clothes'
disguise." She glanced down at her jeans and back at
him.

"It'll help. I'm afraid Edna knows the zoo uniform
much too well."

"Do you think she'll be suspicious if no other people are around?"

"I hope not. She'll be inside the elephant house by this time, so my idea is to place you in the doorway to her section, far enough away so that she has to stretch her trunk and reach to get the cones. If she has to work for it a little, maybe that will allay her suspicions. She'll have the leg chain on, so you won't have to worry about her hurting you."

By the time they arrived at the park, an uncomfortable silence had fallen between them. Cassie's hands felt clammy with nervous perspiration. The tension between them, the emotions that lay just below the surface, were building to an intolerable level.

She followed Paul inside and helped him prepare the ice-cream cones. "You know, if she's as smart as you say she is, it might help to feed the two other elephants first."

"Good idea." He smiled. "You seem to be having more than your share of those today."

She laughed. "Let's go find Edna."

As they approached the elephant exhibit, Paul stopped and handed Cassie the box of cones. "The ones on the top don't have any medication. I'm going to sneak into the elephant house and watch—just in case you run into a problem."

"That's not really necessary. The elephants aren't belligerent. Besides, as you pointed out, they'll be wearing leg chains."

"I don't care. I won't allow you in there alone. It's against our safety rules."

She sighed. "All right,. Where will you be?"

"At the other end of the hall, out of sight."

"Okay." Cassie took the keys from his hands and

entered the building. Standing on the concrete walkway, she peered inside the large rooms that housed the elephants.

She approached with the ice cream, staying far enough away so that they'd have to reach for the cones in her hands.

After feeding the two healthy elephants first, she entered the doorway separating the two rooms and peered anxiously at Edna. "Here you go, girl. I'm sorry you have to be isolated, so you're going to get a few extra." She fed the hungry elephant two untreated cones, then prepared to start with the ones containing the medication.

The instant the third cone reached her mouth, Edna rejected it. Before Cassie had a chance to react, the elephant squirted the entire front of her clothes with medicated caramel-fudge ice cream. Cassie gasped in surprise and stepped back, her eyes glued to the hostile animal. As her heel made contact with the slippery ice cream on the concrete floor, her feet shot out from under her and she landed on her rear end in a pool of melted ice cream.

Within seconds Paul was at her side. "Are you okay?" he asked anxiously.

Clasping his arm for support, she pulled herself painfully erect and limped out of the enclosure. "I think I've broken my entire body. My knee got twisted beneath me when I fell, and my skin feels like a tractor ran over it."

"I'll help you get back to the hospital and we'll take a look."

"No need, Doctor. I'll just go home and put some ice on it."

"Don't be ridiculous. I'll check you over first. If there are any serious injuries, I'll want to file a workman's comp form."

"Forget it. Just take me back to your car, okay?"

"First the hospital."

"I said I'm all right," she insisted.

"Fine. Then you won't mind if I take a look."

"You are so stubborn!" She leaned on him and began hopping toward the hospital.

"Wait a second." He bent to pick her up, but she stiffened abruptly.

"You're not carrying me, and that's final!"

He smiled arrogantly. "Being in my arms affects you that much, does it?"

"Stuff a sock in it, Doctor." She shot him a mirthless smile. "I thought we had agreed to keep our relationship strictly business. Weren't you the one who was worried about conducting ourselves like professionals during working hours?"

His expression turned dark and forbidding. "It's long past regular working hours, Cassie, and I'm tired of playing games." Ignoring her protests, he slung her easily over his left shoulder.

"What are you doing?" she exclaimed shrilly. "I demand you put me down this instant."

"I'm taking you back to the hospital the fastest way I know how, and I'm not putting you down. With you limping and hopping your way there, it would take till morning."

Flailing her arms and legs, she fought the light-headed sensation caused by having her head dangle down. "I hate this! Will you put me down?"

"After all I've done for you?" He gave an exaggerated sigh. "You're an ungrateful little wench, you know that? All I've ever asked from you are three little words that would make me walk on air."

"You've got them: go hang yourself!"

He slapped her buttocks playfully. "Now be nice."

"You're getting to be a real pain, you know that?"

"Of course."

"Paul!"

Chuckling, he carried her into the hospital and directly to their office. He dumped her into the nearest chair, then stood grinning over her. "You were starting to get heavy. If having to carry you around is going to become a habit between us, I suggest you consider going on a diet."

"And I suggest you consider a lobotomy. But since you never listen to me, why should I listen to you?" She ran an exploratory hand over her aching shin.

Paul leaned over and examined the swollen, discolored area. At length he said, "I can't be sure without X rays, but I'm almost certain nothing's broken. It's probably a bad sprain, though."

"I've fallen before, Paul. I'm trying to tell you nothing is wrong."

He shrugged. "A sprain can be fairly serious. In any case, you shouldn't put your weight on that leg for a few days."

"I know that." Her anger was directed as much at herself as at him. "I just can't believe that elephant knew the second I gave her the cone with sulfadiazine! She had already eaten two unadulterated cones. You'd think her taste buds would have been numbed from the cold."

"Edna's a sharp old gal." He pulled several paper towels from a dispenser and handed them to her. "Here. Maybe you can wipe some of that stuff off your shirt with these."

But the towels only smeared the ice cream across the dark blue fabric. She tossed them into the trash. "Forget it. It's useless."

"I'll take you home." He leaned over her, about to

pick her up again, but Cassie stiffened and grabbed the nearest object, which happened to be a stapler. She held it over her head in a menacing gesture. "Don't even think it," she warned. "I'll hop if I have to, but you are *not* going to pick me up again. Is that clear?"

His rich laugh made something vibrate deep inside her. "Whatever you say," he agreed, relenting.

Giving him a haughty look, she hopped down the hall and outside to where his car was parked. When they were well on their way, she broke the silence. "So what's next for Edna?"

"I'll have to try to inject her with penicillin."

"How do you plan to get through that thick hide of hers with one jab of the neddle? And what makes you think she'll let you do it? And while we're on the subject, what are you going to do if she moves at a critical time and the needle breaks?"

"Do you know what I've just discovered?" he asked. "Giving you the power of speech was one of nature's worst blunders."

"I've still made several very good points," she shot back smugly. "You're just upset because you know I'm right."

"I'll figure out something," he grumbled.

"I'll try to come up with a plan by the time I get to work tomorrow morning."

"You're not going to work tomorrow morning."

"Wanna bet?" she challenged.

He pulled into her driveway and gave her a long sideways glance. "I'm going to help you get inside, prepare an ice pack for you, and then I'm going home."

"Don't bother. I can handle it."

He gave her a quelling look. She fell silent once again.

He parked the car and walked around to help her out. "Let's go. I don't intend to discuss this any further."

"How can you? You've used every word you know." She hopped out of the car, appalled at her own rudeness. "Paul, I'm sorry, I'm not really angry you. I'm just very annoyed with myself. Please don't add insult to injury by making me feel helpless."

"How about hapless?" He chuckled softly. "Give me your keys."

"Why?"

"So I can run away, have a duplicate made, and come visit you at our in the morning."

"What?"

He shook his head. "Why do you think, goofy?" He didn't wait for an answer. "I'm going to open the door so you can hobble on in."

"What a charming way you have with words. Do consider a career in journalism if you ever give up veterinary practice."

"I'll keep it in mind." He took the keys from her hand, and accompanied her inside.

She dropped onto the couch. "What a miserable way to end the day."

"You do have an ice pack somewhere, don't you?"

She nodded. "In the bathroom cabinet."

He returned a few minutes later. Placing the icy-cold bag over the swelling, he studied her critically. "Okay?"

"No." She leaned back on the sofa and closed her eyes. "I'd better give you fair warning. Pain sours my normally sweet disposition."

"I'd never have noticed," he said drily.

She closed her eyes again, and he bent over and kissed her. His lips pressed tenderly against hers, deepening slowly as they worked a persuasive magic over her. Reason told her to push him away, but an instinctive need kept her from ending the sweet assault of his mouth on hers. The woman in her gloried in the pressure of his demanding lips, and the passion smoldering just below the surface.

Tearing his mouth away from hers at last, Paul stood looking down at her, his eyes burning with desire. "You're so soft, and you feel so good to touch. Do you see what you do to me?"

Her heart raced wildly. In an instant she conceded defeat in the long battle to resist him. She wanted him. Every nerve in her body tensed, waiting with breathless anticipation. But he shook his head. "I know you want me, Cassie, but I also know you're holding something back. Until you can give all of yourself, I won't make love to you again." And without another word, he turned and left.

Cassie heard the door close behind him. Beset with conflicting emotions, she tried to make sense of everything that had happened. Had Craig truly destroyed her ability to trust another man? Paul had told her he loved her. Why couldn't she accept that and forget his past? Hating herself for not being able to discard all reason and follow the dictates of her heart, she drifted into a restless sleep.

When she woke, it was morning. Her leg throbbed painfully. Sitting up, she placed both feet on the floor. First she'd bathe, then consider how to restore her mobility.

Forty minutes later, she stepped out of the tub. She had just managed to hop to the rack and wrap one of the giant towels around herself when the doorbell rang.

Frozen by indecision, she finally opted to ignore it. By the time she had hopped back to the bedroom, it had rung twice more.

She sat down on the edge of her bed, wishing she had never heard of elephants, much less encountered one called Edna. Determined to stop feeling sorry for herself, she went to the dresser and pulled out a pair of comfortable jeans and a faded Mickey Mouse sweatshirt.

She dropped the towel to the floor and hopped around in search of fresh underwear. Suddenly there was a loud rap at her window just inches away. Startled, she whirled, lost her balance, and fell to the floor.

When she looked up again, no one was there. Swearing revenge on whoever it had been, she stood up painfully.

"Good! You're okay! You scared me witless for a minute there." Cassie started to turn and fell again to the carpeted floor.

"Paul! How in the blazes did you get in here?"

He picked her up gently and set her on the bed. "You left your kitchen door open. I rang the bell, and when you didn't answer I got worried. I jumped your fence and checked your window. When I saw you fall down, I ran to the back door, intending to try it, but you had left it open."

"I do sometimes, when it's hot . . ." she said. Suddenly extremely aware of her nakedness, she pulled a pillow free of the bedcovers and held it in front of her. "Paul, please leave."

He smiled. "Not a chance. Besides, since I don't want you to take another fall, I'm going to dress you."

"Over my dead body."

Ignoring her warning, he picked up her clothes and

brought her undergarments to her. Placing them just out of her reach, he held up her lace panties. "Now be good and cooperate."

She glared at him. "I could raise my foot and kick you halfway to China."

"But you won't for three reasons," he said, beginning to work the material up her leg, lingering provocatively at her thighs. "One, you wouldn't really want to hurt me. Two, you know I've already seen you naked, and one more time isn't going to make the slightest bit of difference. Three"—he lifted her off the bed by looping one arm around her waist and pulled the material up around her hips—"you believe in the simple pleasures of life." He retrieved her bra, a smug grin on his face.

"There's one thing you forgot," she said firmly. "I have a temper that makes Mount St. Helen look tame. If you don't leave this bedroom in three seconds, I'm going to flatten you with this huge brass lamp." Her fingers curled around the object on the nightstand.

He chuckled and bowed with mock gallantry. "Okay. I know when I'm not wanted." He placed her clothing beside her. "I'll wait in the living room."

"If you drive away, I won't miss you."

"I can't do that. I brought breakfast for both of us. I didn't think you should get up to cook a meal."

By the time she made her way into the kitchen a few minutes later, he had already set the table. Two Styrofoam containers were centered on placemats. "I picked up some pancakes. I zapped them in your microwave, so they should be nice and hot now. Have a seat." He held out a chair.

Cassie lowered herself into it. "Paul, why are you doing this to me?"

"I brought you some crutches," he went on. "I broke

my leg last year, and I still had these." He pointed to where they were propped up against the wall. "I adjusted them down to your size." He paused. "Well, I think they're your size. You'll have to check them out."

She took a bite of pancake. She was hungry, and it tasted good—much to her chagrin, since she would have derived a certain pleasure from leaving her food untouched. In her present famished state, however, there was little chance of that. After finishing in record time, she looked up.

"I'm glad to see I rescued you from starvation." Paul's eyes shone with amusement.

"You avoided this question before, so I'm going to ask it again. Why are you doing this to me?"

He picked up the Styrofoam containers and tossed them into the trash. "It's very simple. You see, Cassie, I'm in love with you, and I know you're in love with me. I realize that you intend to try to hide from your own feelings. So, since I disagree wholeheartedly with what you're doing, I've decided to make it as hard for you to do that as I possibly can."

CHAPTER
Ten

CASSIE STARED AT Paul in disbelief, sighed, and then glanced at the crutches. She didn't know what to say. She still couldn't deal with what he was telling her. "Do you really think I need those?" she asked softly.

"You won't let me check you properly, so I can't be sure you don't have a hairline fracture. Still, you have nothing to lose by keeping your weight off that leg. It'll heal faster."

She thought about it for a minute. "Okay. We'll give it a try."

He chuckled.

She looked up warily. "Now what?"

"I noticed that you're pretending not to have heard what I said a few minutes ago."

"Will it do me any good to argue with you?"

He brought the crutches over and helped her fit them under her arms. "Not in the slightest."

"Then I don't think I'm going to waste my time."

"Cold-hearted woman." He moved away as she tried to take a few faltering steps.

Slightly off balance, she teetered precariously. "I think the left crutch is slightly longer than the right one."

He took the crutches from her and held them out in front of him. "You're right. I didn't notice before."

A few minutes later, the crutches adjusted, Cassie headed out to Paul's car. "I must say these will make walking easier."

"Good. That's why I brought them." He slipped behind the wheel.

As they headed toward the zoo, she lapsed into thoughtful silence. She did love Paul, and he certainly wasn't going to let her ignore that fact. She peered at him out of the corner of her eye. Was she strong enough to resist him?

"You're killing me with this heavy silence of yours," Paul said. "Why don't you just tell me what you're thinking?"

"I wasn't thinking of anything in particular," she hedged.

"And if I believe that, you'll be glad to sell me several acres of prime land in Florida—as soon as the tide goes out, right?"

She glanced at him sharply, then laughed. "You never give up, do you?"

"Not when I have so much at stake." His expression was serious. "Besides, I'm an optimist. I believe that sooner or later you'll come to your senses and see me for the great catch I am."

"Great catch?" She brushed her bangs out of her eyes. "I suppose," she admitted at length. "But the same can be said for a boatload of tuna, and I certainly wouldn't want one of those."

"Ah, but I'm more versatile." He grinned roguishly. "My talents are many. I'm a great doorman, as you've seen, and I can be an incredible help dressing, or undressing you—"

"Say one more word, and I'll get hostile," she warned.

"Are you threatening me with bodily harm?"

"Only if I can make sure I'm not accommodating your taste for the unusual." A hint of a smile touched her lips.

Paul drove through the gates leading to the zoo, laughing heartily. "I don't think I'll answer that. I'm going to let you worry about it instead. Besides, now that we're back on the job again, I'm sorry to say, you're safe from my advances. At least for a while."

"Right."

"I'm going to drop you off at the entrance so you won't have far to walk. I'll meet you in the office in a few minutes, okay?"

"Sure."

Cassie entered the hospital area. Perhaps if she could keep kidding around with Paul, she could avoid talking about more serious matters, and still maintain a relaxed atmosphere during work hours.

She was just sitting down at her desk when he entered the room. "I think there's trouble brewing," he said in a quiet voice.

"What do you mean?"

"All the trustees' cars are parked out front. They must be having some sort of meeting." He paused. "What worries me is that none was scheduled."

"That doesn't necessarily mean bad news."

"Maybe."

A light knock sounded on the door, and they both looked up. Paul smiled. "Hi, Deb. I thought you might be stopping by. What's going on?"

"I have some interesting news." She took a seat.

"Should I brace myself?"

"It's not that bad, though it might turn out to be rather inconvenient."

Cassie glanced impatiently from one to the other. "Debbie, if you don't tell us what's going on, I think I'm going to explode from curiosity."

Debbie laughed. "Okay, here it is. Did you know that Dr. Walter Taylor is a new member of our board of trustees?"

"The one who wrote that paper comparing the habits of bison in the wild versus those kept in captivity?"

"The same."

"He's considered quite an authority. His paper was touted as the definitive work on the subject."

"So I understand." She leaned forward. "Well, in addition to serving with our trustees, he's been given permission to work part-time with our curators. That way, he can observe the animals he's studying, as well as gather information from our staff."

Paul nodded. "That sounds like a good arrangement."

"Now thanks to him," she continued, "our zoo has been selected to receive a pair of wisents, a European breed of bison that is almost extinct. From what I understand, these animals are found only in one small area of the Polish–Soviet border."

Paul's expression lightened. "That's great!"

"And that's not all." She glanced at her watch. "But I'll let the board tell you. They asked me to bring you in at nine-thirty, and its almost that now. Let's go."

"The trustees want me at their meeting?" Paul asked suspiciously.

"And Cassie."

"Oh?" Instantly alert, Cassie glanced at Paul.

"Let's go, then." He gave Cassie an encouraging grin. "They probably want to make sure we're equipped to treat the wisents if something goes wrong."

As Debbie led the way down the hall, she tried to set Cassie's mind at ease. "Don't worry about a thing. I know this is the first time you've met this bunch, but they're not nearly as imposing as they look."

Moving awkwardly on the crutches, Cassie didn't feel at all reassured as they entered the conference room. Her eyes darted nervously around. A massive oak table seemed to swallow up the room with its enormous proportions. Four inquisitive faces watched her take a seat beside Paul.

Debbie said, "Dr. Prentiss, may I present Dr. Walter Taylor?"

Standing, he offered her his hand. "My pleasure, Doctor. I've heard a lot about you."

Cassie cringed inside, thinking of all the things he could have heard.

Debbie moved on quickly. "This is Peter Hatfield."

In his late fifties with craggy features, Mr. Hatfield looked like a man accustomed to holding positions of power. "How do you do?" he said stiffly. "I see you had an accident. Nothing serious, I hope."

"Oh, no," she said brightly. "Just a slight fall."

"Marc Nolan," Debbie continued.

Cassie shook his hand. *Finally a friendly face,* she

thought. She smiled, and the man's expression lit up.

"And last but not least," Debbie said with a smile, "this is Erica Talbot."

The elderly woman beamed. Cassie liked her immediately.

As Cassie sat down, leaning the crutches against the table, Mrs. Talbot said, "I'm so glad you're working for us, my dear. It's a relief to know that poor Dr. Kelly finally has some help."

Paul smiled and started to answer, but everyone's attention was diverted as Jonathan Knifing, the zoo's president emeritus, walked into the room.

"Good morning everyone." The senior trustee's voice was resonant and deep. After describing their new acquisition, he said, "The city will finance the enclosure that will be needed, and we'll begin construction immediately. Now my report tells me that the animals have been taken from Berlin via U.S. military transport to an air base just outside London. The problem is that the entire country has been quarantined because of a recent outbreak of anthrax. As I'm sure our doctors can verify"—he glanced at Paul and Cassie—"this is an extremely serious and contagious disease among quadrupeds. The animals are being kept inside makeshift pens in a hangar on the outskirts of the base. They've been there for five days, and already they're starting to show signs of illness. Personally, I think it's due to their confinement, but I'm not qualified to say. But you, Dr. Kelly, are eminently qualified to assess their condition. We would therefore like you to go to England and take charge of this project."

"Mr. Knifing," Paul began, "I'm not sure how much good I can do. International law is very rigid when it comes to this type of situation."

"That's true. However, you can maintain the animals' health so that they'll be strong enough to complete the journey when the time comes. Of course, if you find that the wisents are indeed seriously ill, you'll be in a position to make an objective evaluation and select an appropriate course of action."

Paul nodded. "I certainly couldn't make an accurate diagnosis via the telephone."

"Exactly. And since these animals are a gift from another country, the matter is a sensitive one of some diplomatic importance. That's why I'd like you personally to represent the zoo's interests."

Cassie felt a flood of relief. With Paul gone, maybe she could get him out of her system once and for all. Hearing Knifing clear his throat, she glanced up. To her surprise, he was looking directly at her.

"Dr. Prentiss, because of the political delicacy of this situation, we would also like you to accompany Dr. Kelly and assist him in any way possible. We believe you can benefit greatly from this experience."

Cassie's spirits sank. Paul interjected, "It's impossible for Cassie to accompany me, Mr. Knifing. Someone must stay here to look after our current patients, as well as take charge of any emergencies that might arise."

Although Paul was right—someone did have to keep things running smoothly at the zoo—Cassie was struck cold by the vehemence of his tone. For some reason he was determined that she not go with him.

"This is a very delicate situation, Dr. Kelly," Knifing said. "Appearances must be maintained. It's imperative that we don't offend our foreign friends by treating this matter casually. They expect us to put our 'best foot forward,' so to speak. Our own government considers this gift so important, in terms of future trade agreements and the like, that it has offered to pay all travel expenses."

Paul's eyes flashed with a cold anger that shocked Cassie. "Someone *must* take care of our animals here," he insisted again.

"We have taken the liberty of enlisting two vets from the University in Colorado to fill in for you. Dr. Jordan and Dr. Leslie are well known in this country. I'm sure you agree that they are excellent choices."

Cassie's mouth fell open. Disputing either of those men's veterinary qualifications would be like questioning Albert Einstein's mathematical abilities.

Paul's eyebrows shot up. He paused for a moment, then continued. "Still, they are not as familiar with our animals as Dr. Prentiss is."

"Oh, for heaven's sake, Dr. Kelly! Dr. Prentiss has not been here *that* long!" Knifing's voice had sharpened considerably. "Your concern for our animals is commendable, I'm sure, but we need both of you to take care of the bison!" He handed Paul the airline tickets. "If either of you don't have passports, our government liaison assures us they can be expedited. Your tickets are dated for the day after tomorrow. I trust this won't pose an insurmountable problem." Knifing's tone left no room for argument.

"Will that be all?" Paul regarded Knifing with a gaze that would have shaken a lesser man.

"Yes, Doctor. We know you have business to attend to."

Paul held the door open for Cassie. As he strode down the hall, and she swung herself on the crutches, he muttered an oath.

"I don't suppose you'd consider missing the plane," he suggested.

"Are you crazy?" She looked at him, bewildered.

"What's the matter with you? The two vets Knifing mentioned are among the best in the country. The animals will be well cared for."

"It's totally unnecessary for you to make this trip. I don't need your help."

As they entered the hospital area, Cassie caught and held his gaze, her anger rising. "First you want to be with me all the time and become an indispensable part of my life. Now you want to get thousands of miles away from me. You're about as consistent as the weather."

"You won't be needed."

"The trustees think differently," she shot back. "What is it with you? Do you think I'm going to see a sick bison and faint or something?"

"Or something."

They entered their office, and Cassie shut the door. "All right, I want an explanation. Do you doubt my ability to handle the job?"

He shook his head. "No. but it doesn't matter what I think, since it looks like you're coming anyway. You might as well go get your passport."

"I'm not going anywhere, Paul. Not until you tell me what the hell is going on."

He gave her a tight smile that infuriated her. "Fine. If you can't get your passport in time, they'll have to leave you behind."

"Why?" She hobbled around the room trying to quiet her mounting temper. "Don't tell me you think I can't handle myself around a large exotic. If you do, so help me Paul, I'm going to brain you with the coffee maker."

He slumped into his chair. "Just forget it."

"I won't forget it!" She leaned over his desk. "I want an explanation."

He scowled at her. "A trip of this kind can be very

trying. I don't want to have to worry about you or look after you. I'll have enough on my hands taking care of the animals."

"You've lost your mind." She sat back down and stared at him. "I'll tell you what. Why don't you concentrate very hard and see if you can come up with an explanation that makes some sense."

Obviously angry now, he walked around the desk and stood motionless in front of her. "Do you want the real story? All right, I'll give it to you." He paused, looked away and then back at her. "Two years ago the zoo sent me overseas. We were slated to receive a rare species of monkey from Ceylon that had been bred successfully in England. Instead of risking the animal's survival in transit, they sent me to get it. I took Ruth along. I figured it could be a second honeymoon for us." He walked to the window and stared out. "While we were over there, she caught a rare form of hepatitis. The doctors had no treatment for it. She died about a month later."

Stunned, Cassie swallowed against the lump in her throat. Thoughts ran together in her mind, racing back and forth in a swirl of confusion. "I—"

"You want to know why I don't want you along?" He turned and faced her. "It goes a lot deeper than just bad memories, Cassie. If anything happened to you on this trip, I think I'd..." He paused, struggling with his own emotions, "I lost the first woman I loved." He turned away. "I won't go through that again."

She walked to him and placed her hand on his arm. "Paul..."

His face was expressionless, as if a tight mask had slipped into place. "I'm going to take care of rounds. Go get your passport and start packing." He moved toward the door.

"Paul, wait."

"Cassie, just do it!" She heard his footsteps echo down the hall.

Cassie ran her fingers through her hair as she tried to calm herself.

"Hi." Debbie stood at the doorway.

"Come in." Cassie wanted to project an air of professionalism, but all she could think of was Paul.

Debbie sat down across from her. "He told you about Ruth, didn't he?"

"How did you know?"

"Cassie, Paul and I have been friends for a long time. I hope you won't mind what I'm about to say, but I think I'd better get this out in the open." She hesitated only briefly. "I've been watching you around Paul, and I believe you care a great deal for him."

Cassie nodded. There was no use denying it. "I do."

"If he's difficult to deal with on this trip, try not to judge him harshly. You see, there's something I feel you should know. Something else that I'm certain he hasn't told you."

Cassie's attention was riveted on Debbie.

"Paul's always blamed himself for Ruth's death."

"But that's ridiculous!"

"To you and me, maybe, but not to him. You see, at first she didn't want to go. But he convinced her to accompany him." She held up a hand, halting Cassie's protest. "Since then, Paul has suppressed a lot of guilt. And it's worked—to a degree. He's put his life back together again. The problem is that by refusing to think about his loss, he still hasn't come to terms with it. This trip might turn out to be the catalyst that forces him to examine everything that happened. But until he works it out in his own mind, he's going to go through hell."

"But it isn't his fault that Ruth died."

"I'm sure he'll reach that conclusion by himself in time." Debbie paused. "If you can help him see it sooner, you'll be sparing him a lot of heartache. I think Paul feels ready to start a new life. But as long as the past is hanging over him, he'll never be really free to live fully once again." She regarded Cassie earnestly. "Do you understand what I'm saying?"

"I understand, and I promise to see what I can do."

Cassie fought a sinking feeling in the pit of her stomach. Maybe she *could* show Paul that his guilt was misplaced. But by doing so, wouldn't she increase her own involvement with him? And what then? Would she be able to accept him, knowing that the love he felt for Ruth was so deep that the memory of their years together would never truly fade from his mind?

CHAPTER
Eleven

PREPARING FOR THE trip kept her busy, and Cassie saw little of Paul in the next day and a half. Fortunately, her leg improved and she could walk easily without crutches. It wasn't until she found herself seated next to Paul on the plane that she once again questioned the wisdom of coming along. Could she have refused to go without jeopardizing her job? Probably not, she conceded. Yet her emotions were confused as she speculated on the possible outcome of the trip.

"So we're finally on our way," she said at length.

He nodded. "It's as if we've lived two lifetimes in the past forty-eight hours."

She wondered what he meant. Had it been so difficult

for him, or was he simply referring to the hectic pace of the last couple of days?

"There were times when I wasn't sure either one of us would make it on such short notice," she said.

"Rest assured that Knifing would have placed us on this flight even if he had to carry us on his back to the airport. When that man gets an idea in his head, he's as inflexible as the Rock of Gibraltar."

"I get the feeling you've had differences of opinion before." She paused, then added, "Yet I'd be willing to bet you've won your share of the confrontations."

He shrugged. "He might be the Rock of Gibraltar, but you'd be surprised what one determined man with a chisel can do."

She watched as he stared out the window. What was he really thinking? Would he open up and talk about Ruth? How could she help him?

"I wonder what we'll find when we get there."

He gave her a puzzled look. "England."

She laughed. "I was referring to the condition of the animals."

He smiled. "I wouldn't expect too much if I were you. They're trapped with a bunch of airmen who don't have the foggiest notion of what to do with them. Can you imagine the conversations?" He faked a cockney accent: "Say, Alfie, old chum, these beasts are going to need to run about sooner or later. Do you think you could scout up a rather large leash?"

"I get the picture," Cassie said, genuinely amused. "By the way, I didn't get a chance to ask you about Edna."

"I gave her the shot, but I must say it took a bit of ingenuity. I had Pete fill a bucket with apples. She likes them, and she doesn't get them often. Pete kept her busy while I injected her with the penicillin. All I needed was about fifteen seconds to get the needle into the soft skin underneath her foreleg."

"I can't believe she stood still!"

"She probably wouldn't have if she hadn't been feeling so weak from the infection." He shrugged. "Anyway, I checked her before we left, and she's doing just fine."

They lapsed back into silence. Cassie feigned sleep, seeking to escape the tension between them. Every once in a while she stole quick glances at him.

"I know you're not asleep," he said quietly. "Would you like to talk about it?"

She sat up slowly. "No, but I think we'd better."

"Look, the reasons I didn't want you along have little to do with you. I just have to work out a few things in my mind, and the last of my worries is our business relationship."

Against her better judgment she blurted, "If you still have Ruth so fresh in your mind, how could you possibly consider committing yourself to a relationship with me?"

He looked surprised. "I'm not still in love with Ruth, Cassie." His eyebrows furrowed tightly. "Is that what you've been thinking?"

She didn't know how to answer. "I was just curious. Your attitude seems to indicate that you still have strong feelings for her."

"I'll always have strong feelings for her. We spent a long time together. You don't really expect me to forget all of that, do you?"

"No, I don't." There was a finality to her tone that made him look at her quizzically.

"Wait a minute." He shook his head. "Let's stop playing games, all right? Why don't you tell me what's really on your mind."

Instinct told her it was time to change the subject and change it fast. "If I'm acting wierd, it's because I'm the worst traveler you'll ever meet. Did you know I hate planes, I hate flying. In fact, I hate anything that can't be done on the ground."

He laughed. "Trust me. There's nothing to be afraid of. Try not to think of this as a two-hundred-ton hunk of metal that has the audacity to propel itself where it doesn't belong."

"Thanks for the comforting words!" She chuckled softly.

"You're not really scared of flying, are you?" He gave her a speculative look.

"Not afraid, exactly," she ventured hesitantly. "I'm just not comfortable with it."

"How can you say that?" he teased. "Doesn't my wonderful presence soothe your ruffled nerves and calm your fears?"

"No," she replied slowly, "but it does heighten my motion-sickness symptoms."

"Are you trying to say I make you nauseous?"

She nodded, grinning, relieved to be avoiding more serious discussion.

Something in his smile suggested that he, too, was content to keep things light. "You know, you really should count your blessings. You're extremely lucky to be in love with a man who knows how to be patient when you play hard to get."

She closed her eyes and shook her head. If only it were that simple! "Oh, really?" She tried hard to maintain the spirit of their game.

"You might as well admit it," he teased. "You've been in love with me right from the start. In fact, you probably ran into my car deliberately, just so I'd pay attention to you."

"Maybe I should move to another seat. That way I won't disturb your fantasies," she suggested.

"Don't. Being all alone is definitely not part of my fantasy. Although being alone *with you* appeals to me. Care to step into a private nook at the back of the plane?"

"Paul!" She glanced quickly around the cabin. "For heaven's sake! What if someone heard you?"

"They'd take one look at you and understand completely." He reached for her hand.

"Take a walk, will you!" she said with a mock growl.

"I know my presence leaves you confused, dear Cassie, but I can't go far in these circumstances. " He indicated their cramped quarters.

It was a long flight. Although she tried to keep up the cheery banter, every once in a while Cassie caught the haunted look in Paul's eyes. By the time they arrived at Heathrow, she'd made up her mind. No matter what the cost, she would do everything in her power to help him. She cared for him too much to allow him to continue punishing himself.

It was late in the afternoon when they finally disembarked. A young man in a military uniform greeted them at the gate.

"Hello. I'm Sergeant Jenkins." He shook their hands. "I've been instructed to drive you to our base."

Surprised, Cassie asked, "How in the world did you know who we were?" Then she smiled sheepishly as she glanced down at her medical bag. "Oh, never mind."

Sergeant Jenkins laughed. "Actually, my captain showed me a couple of photographs that had been telexed over when he briefed me."

After they cleared customs, the serviceman led the way outside to a government car parked nearby. A cold drizzle was falling, making Cassie glad to step into the warm car. After checking to be sure their luggage was secure in the trunk, Sergeant Jenkins slipped behind the wheel.

Cassie whispered to Paul, "Boy, this is some service!"

"It's called the Air Force."

She poked him lightly in the ribs. "I mean getting picked up at the airport, being recognized on sight, and all that."

"They consider us V.I.P.'s, so let's not blow our cover. Once they find out we're just ordinary people, we'll probably have to walk back to the airport."

"Your first time in England?" Sergeant Jenkins asked.

"Yes, it is." Cassie's enthusiasm was hard to disguise.

"Then I'll drive through London instead of around it. That'll give you a chance to see some of the sights."

Twenty minutes later, as they maneuvered down the left side of crowded London streets, Cassie was exhilarated. It was all so different and exciting! They passed modern high-rises and centuries-old churches. She caught glimpses of green squares surrounded by elegant town houses, and long rows of gray cottages. Soon they were speeding along the Thames, past the Tate Gallery, Parliament, and Big Ben, then down another wide avenue to Trafalgar Square, where hundreds of pigeons flew into the air at once, adding drama to the National Gallery and Lord Nelson's statue. In minutes they were passing beautiful St. James's Park and Buckingham Palace, then traveling north and west to Hyde Park and Kensington Gardens. Cassie exclaimed over such greenery in the midst of the busy city, and took delight in pointing out the red double-decker buses.

All too soon, just as the sun began to sink, they headed out into the countryside. Cassie found herself wishing for just a few more hours of daylight. Everything was so new to her that she didn't want to miss a single sight.

She couldn't help comparing the rolling green of the mist-shrouded countryside to the desert she'd left behind in New Mexico. There were more shades of green here than she had ever seen before. Raindrops glistened with silvery light as they fell on the leaves of the trees and ran in rivulets down the side of the road. Cassie's eyes widened as they passed a field covered with bluebells.

Since Paul didn't seem in the mood for conversation, she kept silent too. Perhaps the key to erasing the pain of his memories was to replace them with happier new ones. Content for the moment with that possibility, she leaned back and watched the landscape outside her window.

It was dark by the time the sergeant drove through the gates of the base. "Here we are," he announced.

They entered a residential area lined with identical red brick houses and pulled into a narrow gravel driveway. "This is your cottage," Sergeant Jenkins informed them. He parked the car and escorted them to the door. "It has three bedrooms, so I'm sure you'll find it adequate. We do apologize for not being able to get you separate cottages, but we have other visiting dignitaries and all of our other housing is already occupied."

Cassie stepped inside with a sense of renewed tension. She hadn't realized she'd have to share sleeping quarters with Paul. The situation was bound to cause problems.

The living room was comfortably decorated. Linen draperies in a rich chocolate color covered the windows, and two pale gold sofas provided adequate seating.

Suddenly feeling very tired, Cassie said, "There's no

need to apologize, Sergeant. This is lovely."

"Yes, we're both grateful," Paul added.

After bringing in their luggage, Sergeant Jenkins gave them a snappy salute. "Tomorrow, after you've had a chance to check the animals, Commander Blackwell would like you both to have lunch with him."

"We'd be honored," Paul said.

"Then I'll tell him you accept. Is there anything else I can do for you?"

Cassie suppressed a yawn. "No, but thanks for asking."

As soon as he left, she collapsed on the sofa while Paul walked down the hall. "You know, I didn't realize how tired I was until now." She stretched.

Paul reappeared. "Which room do you want? Gentleman that I am, I'll let you choose."

"I want one with a bed."

"Funny." He took her suitcase down the hall. "The master bedroom has its own bath," he called. "Why don't you take that one?"

"Fine." She followed him, grateful that he was cooperating, yet unable to repress a twinge of regret at the ease with which he seemed to control whatever remained of his desire for her.

"I'll take the bedroom down the hall," he continued. "If we're going to coexist, I think we'd better give each other a little breathing space." He set her suitcase on a luggage caddy inside her room.

She rubbed her eyes and plopped down on the edge of the bed. "Thanks for bringing my suitcase in. Good night."

"Want me to tuck you in?"

Although her eyes were closed, she caught the teasing note in his voice and smiled. "Want me to punch you?"

"Are you sure there isn't anything you want me to do for you before I leave? I could help you undress."

She laughed wearily. "Will you get out of here!"

He leaned over and kissed her lightly. "Good night, pretty lady." Then he left, closing the door quietly.

Cassie rose to slip out of her clothes, allowing them to drop onto the carpet. She tossed back the covers and crawled between the sheets. Within seconds. she was fast asleep.

The next sound she heard was a light rapping on her door. "Cassie?"

She stretched lazily. "All right, I'm up."

"Hurry. You don't want breakfast to get cold," Paul called.

"What breakfast? Don't tell me you cooked!" She tossed the covers back and jumped out of bed.

"They brought a real English breakfast: corn flakes and milk, fried eggs with tomatoes, toast and tea."

"All that? Okay, I'll be right out." She pulled a robe from her suitcase along with her toothbrush and toothpaste, and headed for the bathroom. When she emerged minutes later, her face was made up and her hair combed neatly.

Paul looked up from the kitchen table. "You didn't have to put your makeup on. You're beautiful without it."

"How would you know?" she teased. She sat across the table from him and buttered a piece of toast.

He chuckled. "Remember the night you slept over at my place? That morning when you thought I was sleeping and dashed into the bathroom to fix yourself up?"

"Yes, I remember. You were sound asleep."

"I had gotten up earlier. You looked so peaceful and innocent sleeping all curled up."

She sighed. "Are you implying that I'm not innocent?"

"Leave it to you to turn a compliment into an insult."

She laughed. Then as the intimacy of the setting began to make her feel uncomfortable, she ate in silence, finishing the last of her eggs and turning the conversation back to business, "Do you know where they're keeping our bison?"

"No, not really. But when the airman brought breakfast he said that someone would be by to pick us up at nine. From what I understand, they made a pen of sorts in an empty hangar."

"That doesn't sound too bad."

"The problem is that the animals weren't let out of the crates until twenty-four hours after their arrival. It seems they expected to ship them out at any moment. Finally, when the British government didn't okay the papers they needed, they gave up."

"But this is a U.S. base. I thought the British didn't have jurisdiction here."

"They don't. Not really. It's just a question of diplomatic courtesy." He finished another piece of toast. "Actually, I think it's more than that. I'd be willing to bet our own government was afraid the animals might be carrying disease."

"They could have quarantined them through normal channels."

"I think they were planning to quarantine them here, and then again after they reached the States."

"That's ridiculous! They can't keep those animals confined forever and expect them to remain healthy."

"That's probably why we're here, to keep the wisents healthy while everyone else exercises their paranoia."

"If you're right, we can't just play along. We've got to do something."

"I agree." He finished his tea. "But the first order of business is to check out the animals."

As Cassie stood up, Paul put his hand over hers. Her senses cartwheeled. "Just one more thing." She looked at him, hating the way her heart leaped into her throat every time he touched her. "We're here as a team, but I'm still responsible for your safety. I don't want you to go off without me, whether on a sightseeing tour or to check the animals. Is that clear?"

She started to tell him that she didn't work twenty-four hours a day and that her time was her own, but then she remembered what had happened to Ruth. Was this his way of trying to make sure nothing happened to her? She softened her expression. "Are you sure you can handle *that* much togetherness?" she asked lightly, trying to tease him out of his somber mood.

It didn't work. "I can handle it."

Fighting the urge to run into his arms, to hold him and tell him how much he meant to her, she took his hand in both of hers and squeezed gently. "It'll be all right, Paul."

Alarm flickered briefly in his eyes, and then it was gone. Once again he gave her a roguish grin. "By the way, don't feel you have to look your best around me all the time. We're not always at work, you know. You didn't even have to wear a robe this morning. You could have eaten breakfast in your pajamas."

"Oh, no, I couldn't." She smiled back. If he wasn't ready to talk about his fears, she wouldn't pressure him.

"Why not?"

"I wasn't wearing any." Without a backward glance, she sauntered down the hall and into the bedroom.

CHAPTER
Twelve

WHEN SERGEANT JENKINS arrived, Cassie was ready to go. Paul locked up the house and slipped into the seat beside her.

"By the way, Doctors, I forgot to mention something last night. I'm to be at your disposal if you want to take any excursions into the countryside."

Cassie's eyes lit up, but Paul's face remained impassive. "Thank you, Sergeant. We'll let you know." He paused, then added, "By the way, how long have the animals been here?"

"A little over a week, sir."

"And when did they start showing signs of illness?"

"Actually, sir, only one of them is acting strangely. Of course, with the roar of the jet engines going right over them, they're a bit nervous. They aren't eating much, which may be why the smallest one is acting so lethargic."

"Have any of the local vets checked them out?"

"No, sir. We were told you were coming, so we just waited. But our flight surgeon here on base paid them a visit. He checked them for anthrax while they were still in their crates."

"And?"

"They didn't show any traces of it." He chuckled. "I'll tell you one thing. Doc much prefers his human patients. He was a bit edgy around the animals."

"It takes a while to get used to them," Cassie admitted, recalling her own experiences.

The base was larger than Cassie had supposed. The minute they left the residential area, they entered a maze of winding streets. Turning down Q Street, they traversed a large open expanse of countryside. Green fields seemed to go on forever. A gray mist hung over the land.

"It's beautiful in an eerie sort of way," Cassie said.

"That's because this side of the base is so empty. Most of the expansion and construction has taken place on the west side."

"The hangar must really be in an isolated spot," Paul said absently.

"Yes, it is. We figured it was safer that way, in case one or both of the wisents managed to get out."

Sergeant Jenkins headed the vehicle down a well-worn, bumpy road and parked in front of a row of dilapidated, steel-framed buildings. As Cassie stepped out of the car, she noted the disrepair of the concrete runway. Large potholes dotted it from one end to the other. "No wonder it's deserted!" she exclaimed.

The sergeant laughed. "You ought to see the others." He pointed to a hangar located just a few feet away. "They're in there."

It was impossible to mistake the bellowing sounds emerging from the building. "They're penned up, right?" Paul verified.

"Yes sir, but I'd better warn you. They have a way of crashing through the barriers we set up and giving themselves the run of the entire hangar. I suppose we should consider ourselves lucky. At least they haven't figured out how to break out of the hangar yet."

Paul and Cassie exchanged wary glances. "We better not take any risks," Paul said. "We'll slip inside once we have our CO_2 guns ready."

After preparing their equipment, they tugged open the door and cautiously entered the hangar. The animals had indeed escaped their pen and taken over the entire domed enclosure. Taller than their American cousins, the wisents stood over six feet high at the shoulder. With their dark faces and shaggy light brown fur, topped with curved horns, they looked like giant buffaloes from the Old West, except that these bison originated in Lithuania, not Wyoming.

Hearing them enter, the larger bison glanced toward them, then wandered off in the opposite direction. The smaller one lay on the concrete floor, scarcely moving.

"They don't seem nervous," Paul whispered.

"There are no jets flying overhead right now."

"Good point. Let's get this over with, then." Taking aim, they lodged their darts in the animals' hindquarters. The larger one bellowed and turned to face them. For several seconds it stood staring at them.

Paul and Cassie remained immobile. At length, losing

interest, the animal turned and walked away.

"Let's get out of here," Paul urged. "The tranquilizer won't take effect for another twenty minutes or so, and it isn't safe to stick around."

As they stepped outside, Cassie said, "Either they're very placid animals, or they're really sick."

"They're not an aggressive breed. In fact, they were hunted almost to extinction during the 1920's. They're peaceful animals who are happy to wander along in the forest feeding on oak, elm, and willows. They might come toward us out of curiosity, but they won't charge unless they feel threatened. From what I've read, you'd have to corner one or come near its young before it would be willing to fight."

"Poor creatures. No wonder they were almost killed off."

"Mind you, they aren't exactly tame either," he cautioned her.

"Oh, I realize that." Cassie checked her watch. "Shall I take a look and see how they're doing?"

Paul verified the time. "Let's both go."

"Is it okay if I come along too?" Sergeant Jenkins asked.

Cassie gave Paul a quick glance. At his nod, she said, "Sure, come on. Just stay a discreet distance away."

Both animals were sleeping peacefully when they entered the spacious hangar. Cassie glanced at the smaller bison. "Let me take that one."

"You're always for the underdog." Paul chuckled softly as he stooped next to the larger animal and removed a stethoscope from his bag.

He finished before Cassie and stood watching her. "Can I help?"

"I don't know. She pressed against the animal's swollen abdomen and felt carefully as she released it. "I'm pretty sure this female's...On second thought, come take a look and tell me what you think."

After checking the wisent's heart and vital signs, Paul made a rectal examination and looked at Cassie with amazement. "She's pregnant."

"That's what I thought."

"You realize this is going to complicate matters. As rare as these animals are, we can't afford to lose the calf. The mother certainly shouldn't stay here any longer than is absolutely necessary."

"But the entire country is under quarantine. How do we fight that?" Cassie asked.

"We're scheduled to have lunch with the base commander. We'll ask him."

Cassie made a few notes on her pad. "This bison is going to need a lot more high-protein food and more water. She's dehydrated."

"So's mine. I think he's suffering from a slight case of malnutrition. Once we get him on a balanced diet, though, he should be fine."

"I think I know how we might get them to reduce the restrictions that are keeping the animals from completing their journey. Since we don't know much about this breed, we're going to have to do a little 'in the field' experimenting before we can find the right diet. And that's going to require careful supervision by zoo employees."

Paul's eyes strayed to the large male. "Maybe we can also add a gentle reminder that the pair is a gift to the U.S. from a not very friendly foreign country."

Cassie nodded enthusiastically. "What you're saying, then, is that we should point out to the commander that if anything happens to these animals, it's going to reflect badly on us, as well as on him."

"That's about it."

Cassie checked her watch. "Let's move to the far end of the hangar and make sure they wake up all right."

As the animals began to stir, Cassie and Paul lapsed into quiet thought. Finally Cassie said, "The female seems to be about a quarter of the way through her pregnancy. What do you think?"

Paul watched as the male struggled to his feet. "I'd say so, from the sound of the heartbeat. But judging from her weight, I don't think the calf is going to be very large."

"I don't either." She paused. "Do you think she'll carry it to term?"

"I'm not sure. We'll have to wait and see. This trip can't be too easy on her."

Cassie went to the door and glanced outside. "England is so beautiful. I wish we had more time to look around. Have you ever been here on vacation?"

"Sure. Several times, actually, with—" He pursed his lips into a thin line. "The animals will be all right now. Let's get out of here."

How could she get him to tell her about Ruth? There had to be a way to get him to open up to her!

"We're going to have to do a little sightseeing," she said. "There's no way I'm going back home without seeing some of this country first."

He nodded absently. "I'll see what I can do. The animals won't need round-the-clock care, so we should have time."

Sergeant Jenkins came hurrying toward them. "I'm sorry I'm late. I just thought I'd take a little walk while you two were busy. I hope I haven't kept you long."

Paul shook his head. "We've just been looking around. It's so peaceful out here."

"Peaceful?" He gave them both a knowing smile. "Maybe right now, but the minute the fighter squadrons take off for their daily hops, the noise will be deafening."

Cassie was worried. "The animals, particularly the female, shouldn't be subjected to that sort of stimulus."

"Explain it to the commander," Jenkins suggested. "That will strengthen your case for clearing the animals to leave as soon as possible."

Paul rubbed his palm against his chin. "Let's head back to our cottage. We both need to shower and get ready for that lunch."

"How formal is this?" Cassie asked as she slipped inside the car.

"You'll be at the Officers' Club inside the commander's private dining room," Jenkins answered. "A dress or a skirt would be fine."

Paul leaned toward her. "I'm not sure what I brought with me. I hope I tossed in a pair of regular slacks."

They parked in front of their cottage, and Jenkins opened the door for them. "I'll be right here when you're ready."

Thanking him, they went inside. Moments later Paul emerged from his bedroom. "I'm saved," he called. "I did bring a pair of black slacks."

"Good. I sure hope there's enough hot water for both of us."

Paul bolted into the bathroom, and seconds later she heard the sound of running water. She waited for him to finish before taking her own shower.

Twenty minutes later, she met him in the living room. She was wearing a white blouse decorated with delicate embroidery, and a dark green linen skirt that fit smoothly over her hips.

Paul let out a wolf whistle. "That's a terrific outfit. Are you sure you want to wear it around a military base?"

"Are you kidding? Who's going to start anything when I'm sitting with the base commander?"

"Me."

"You, I can handle."

As the Sergeant drove them to the club, Cassie tried to collect her thoughts. She was having fun with Paul, but it was obvious that both of them were avoiding certain subjects. She sighed softly. Sooner or later she would have to work up enough courage to ask him about Ruth. She made up her mind to broach the subject as soon as possible. The longer she allowed it to remain hidden beneath the surface, the more difficult it would become.

As they strolled into the club, a tall, imposing man approached them. He had salt-and-pepper hair and hazel eyes. Sergeant Jenkins introduced them to Commander Blackwell, saluted the commander, and left.

The officer led the way into the dining room and they sat down at a round table by the windows. A young waiter, impeccably attired in white, handed them menus.

Paul was sitting across the table from her. For an instant their eyes met. He smiled, and the world seemed transformed. Acutely aware of his physical presence, of his hand resting on the table and his knees almost touching hers beneath it, she had to look away. What was it about Paul that dwarfed the men around him? For a moment she had felt herself sinking into his deep blue eyes.

A memory stirred. She recalled the last time he had looked at her in that penetrating way of his . . . Taking a sip of water, she chided herself silently. What a time to allow her imagination to misbehave! Her hand was trembling as she set her glass down.

"I've always had a special interest in animals," the commander was saying. "I read up on these bison of yours, and I'm amazed that they were given to us. They're almost extinct, you know."

Cassie nodded and glanced at Paul. He was still looking at her with a steady, unblinking gaze. It was impossible to ignore the effect he was having on her. Struggling to control her rioting emotions, she made a great show of listening to the commander.

"Tell me Cassie, do you agree with my theory?" he asked.

She blinked. What had he said?

Paul's eyes danced. "Actually, sir, neither of us have had much experience with these animals. We know their basic nutritional requirements, but as to what specific foods they would actually prefer to eat, we're just as much in the dark as anyone else. My idea is simply to experiment until we find a diet that meets their needs as well as their tastes."

Silently thanking Paul, Cassie added, "That's one of the reasons we want to get the animals to the States as soon as possible. We have an excellent staff at our zoo. In addition, we have the nation's top authority on bison. He'll certainly be able to advise us on how to make the animals' transition to captivity less traumatic."

After they'd glanced though the menus and ordered, Paul picked up the conversation. "Actually, Commander, we have a problem. This morning we discovered that the female is pregnant."

Commander Blackwell's eyebrows rose in surprise. "What's the problem? Surely, that'll be a bonus for your zoo."

"We're very pleased," Cassie agreed. "Unfortunately, we're also very worried. The female must be kept relatively free of stress, and the jets . . ." She let the sentence hang.

"I see what you're getting at," the commander said slowly. "We really don't want anything to happen to such a valuable gift, particularly when it comes from a country that hasn't been particularly friendly to us in the past."

Paul nodded. "I've been concerned about the diplomatic repercussions."

"I'll see what I can do," the commander said at length. Paul and Cassie exchanged hopeful glances. "I might be able to get in touch with a few friends who can look into this matter for us." He paused thoughtfully as the waiter placed their food in front of them. "Yes, I just might be able to help you. With a little luck, you should be on your way in no time."

"We'd really appreciate it, Commander," Paul replied.

"I'll be in touch with you at around six this evening."

Paul paced up and down the living room, glancing impatiently at his watch. "Just our luck: we have the entire afternoon off, and Jenkins gets called away on urgent business."

"They did say we could have a car from the motor pool." Cassie said.

"They also said they'd deliver it when it was ready. I don't see one outside, do you?" His voice was taut.

"It'll come." She patted the seat beside her. "Come and sit by me. We can use this time to talk."

"We've been talking." He continued to pace.

"Not about the things that really matter, Paul. Let's

stop hiding behind small talk, okay?"

He stopped pacing and faced her. "I think I know where this conversation is heading, Cassie, and I don't want to discuss it."

"Come sit by me."

"Cassie." He shook his head.

"Please," she said, not relenting. After a moment's hesitation, he complied. He leaned back against the cusions and stretched his legs out in front of him.

"Paul, tell me about Ruth," Cassie said softly.

"There's nothing to tell. She was my wife and she died."

"Paul."

"Is this really important to you? Because I ought to tell you I don't enjoy going over the past." His voice was harsh.

"It *is* important to me."

"Why?"

"Because I care about you, and to understand you I need to know about your past." She had spoken the words before she realized just how true they really were.

He studied her thoughtfully. "All right, Cassie. You're the woman I love, and I guess that gives you the right to know. Where do you want me to start?"

"How did you fall in love with her?"

"I met her the year I graduated from college." His voice softened. "It was a good marriage. Oh, we had our problems like anyone else, but all in all they were good years. About the only source of contention we ever had was my job. She thought I should go into private practice. What she resented most was the time it required. In those days we didn't have a large staff. I had to take charge of virtually everything that involved the animals, from raising them to maintaining their health.

"Poor Ruth was always planning vacations and having to cancel them at the last minute because of some emergency or another. It was hard for her. In the four years we were married we were never really able to get away. That's why I talked her into going to England with me to pick up the monkey that the game preserve was donating to our zoo. I thought we could make the trip a second honeymoon. I thought I was doing this wonderful thing for her." His fists clenched and his throaty laugh echoed with bitterness. "It was so wonderful that it ended up killing her."

"Paul, it wasn't your fault," Cassie said resolutely.

"Fault?" He shrugged. "It's not a matter of fault, Cassie, it's a matter of regret. There are so many things I'd do differently if I could do them all over again. There are so many words I left unsaid." He turned to her in surprise. "It's my past that bothers you, isn't it? That's what's really been on your mind all along!" As the realization dawned, his expression softened. "You haven't been honest with me, have you?"

"I..." She started to deny it, but the lump in her throat made speech impossible.

"Cassie, you should have told me this before." He touched her cheek in a gentle caress. "Go ahead and ask me anything you want to know."

"But I'm supposed to be helping you..." She faltered.

"Me?"

"I thought you were blaming yourself for Ruth's death."

He shook his head. "No. Oh, maybe right after she died, but the hardest part was dealing with the feeling that life had cheated us. We had so many plans, so many things we never had a chance to do or experience together. Those thoughts ate me alive. In time, though, I learned to accept it."

"But don't you see? Everything's still too fresh in your mind. You're still in love with her, Paul." Cassie's voice trembled, but she quickly brought herself back under control.

"In love?" He shook his head. "I'll always remember her, but she's more like a memory that's become a part of me now. You're right about one thing, though. I am in love." His smile was tender. "With you."

Cassie felt warmed to the core by his intense gaze and gentle words, but the conversation left her feeling more confused than enlightened. He'd turned many of her assumptions upside down, and she couldn't assimilate this new picture of his relationship with Ruth.

A knock sounded on the door and Paul stood up. "Think about it, Cassie, and we'll talk more later."

Trying to sort out her jumbled thoughts, she watched him open the door and take a set of car keys from a young airman. They exchanged a few words about the car.

After the serviceman left, Paul's eyes swept over her face. "I wish you had been honest with me from the beginning," he said. "Didn't you trust me?"

"It wasn't that," she said, regaining her voice. "I had to get things clear in my own mind first."

"There's a lot more to this than your concern that I still might have feelings for Ruth, isn't there?"

"Yes." Her eyes held his. For the first time she followed the dictates of her heart without hesitation. "I have kept certain things from you, but the time for secrets is over. Let's go for a drive, and I'll tell you the rest."

CHAPTER
Thirteen

THE MINUTE THEY left the base, the landscape became decidedly British. Half-timbered houses and thatched cottages were nestled among rolling hillsides, and green fields were bordered by thick hedgerows.

Paul glanced at Cassie as he drove. "You said you wanted to talk."

"I know, but it's more difficult than I thought."

They crossed a stone bridge and entered a small village where houses and shops of weathered brick fronted narrow streets. "Let's go for a walk," Paul suggested.

"Yes, I'd like that."

As they parked beside a stone church whose spire reached high into the blue sky, Paul said, "Come on, pretty lady. We'll relax and get to the heart of whatever's bothering you."

With her hand tucked safely in his, they strolled past charming cottages, stopping occasionally to peer inside shop windows. At the edge of town they spotted a pony grazing in a nearby field. "It's so tranquil," Cassie murmured. "I just want to enjoy it. I don't want to have to think about anything right now."

They walked down a simple footpath until they came to a gated fence. Paul took Cassie's arm and turned her to face him. "We've avoided this discussion long enough, Cassie. Now tell me what's going on inside your head."

She sighed and urged him across a meadow to a small pond. "I promise I won't put if off any longer. We'll just sit on the ground and talk."

"All right."

Cassie made herself comfortable in the thick grass, and Paul lay on his stomach beside her. "We're here. Now talk to me."

She laughed lightly. "Impatient, aren't you?"

"Cassie!"

"All right, all right!" She took a deep breath and, holding her knees against her chest, began. "What I told you about Craig was true. He did hurt me a great deal. Maybe that's why I'm being so cautious now. I don't want to go through that pain again. You see, I'm not quite sure what to believe anymore. You say you're not in love with Ruth, yet the morning after you made love to me, I saw you pick up her picture from the floor. The pain I saw on your face, the way you looked at that portrait . . . you can't tell me she means nothing to you."

"I never said that," he corrected. "What I did tell you

was that I'm in love with you."

"But your feelings for her are still there."

"I'll always have my memories of her, Cassie. I'd be lying if I told you differently. But I'm not using you as a substitute, if that's what you're worried about." He paused. "I don't know if I can make you understand, but I'll try. When Ruth died, I wanted to die too. But I didn't. A long time later I met you. From the first day, I knew you were special. I didn't want to fall in love with you, but I did. For a while I thought if I just made love to you once, I'd get you out of my system. But it didn't work that way. I held you in my arms and knew there'd be no turning back. I was in love with you, and in return, I wanted you to love me freely and without reservation. But I don't think you can until you understand the way it is between us."

He touched her face lightly. "Ruth will always have a special place in my heart, but that doesn't lessen my feelings for you. I'm not the same person who married Ruth years ago. The experiences that have brought me to this point in my life have changed me, molded me into the man I am today. Ruth was an important part of my past, and her death and my acceptance of it changed me. If you truly love me, you'll understand that the past helped make our present possible."

"I know what you're saying," Cassie said softly, "but understanding intellectually and understanding emotionally are two different things. I want to trust you, to love you without holding back, but I'm afraid."

"Oh, Cassie." He took her hand in his and pressed a kiss into her palm. "It all comes down to this: if you love me, then let your heart show you the way." He stood up and offered her a hand. "I think we should go back now."

A terrible iciness gripped Cassie as they drove back to the base. It was as if the rational part of her had stopped functioning. She was afraid to trust him, yet she might lose him if she didn't break down the barriers that kept her away from him. Was she being selfish in wanting a man whose memories of the past would not serve as a basis of comparison with the future?

Yet the past didn't change her love for Paul. There was no escaping it. She must choose between a life with him on his terms, and a life without him. The dilemma pulled her apart, leading her in two different directions.

Cassie paced the living room early that evening. Paul hadn't said a word to her since they'd left the pond. The tension between them was almost unbearable.

As she waited for the base commander's call, she continued to wrestle with her problem. Paul expected a commitment from her. He had every right to ask for one.

If only there hadn't been a Ruth! Cassie loved Paul, but that love was preventing her from accepting the part of him that belonged to Ruth. She wanted all of him for herself. Yet he'd told her she had all his love. He'd told her that the life he had shared with Ruth, and then her death, had changed him. Suddenly she understood that he was the sum total of all his experiences, and Ruth was part of that experience. Ruth was part of what Paul was today, part of the man she, Cassie, loved.

With a sense of wonder, Cassie examined the simple truth. The realization came to her with great certainty. Why hadn't she seen it before? Paul had told her, yet somehow she had shut out the words.

As understanding dawned, a great sweetness of spirit enveloped her. Ruth was no longer a separate entity. She wasn't 'the other woman.' She was simply a memory that had become a part of Paul—another facet of the complex whole that made him the wonderful man he was today.

Feeling as if she were walking on air, Cassie was about to call for him when a knock sounded on the door. She answered it.

Commander Blackwell stood in the doorway, waving several documents triumphantly in the air. "You're all set!" he announced.

Paul met them in the living room. "What's this?"

"You've been cleared to leave with the animals. There's a military transport scheduled for take off in a hour and a half. It'll take you back to the States, providing you're ready on time."

Paul glanced at Cassie, who nodded in agreement. "We'll make it."

"I've also arranged for you to have access to the animals' compartment during the flight."

"Good," Paul answered. "That way we can keep an eye on the female."

Commander Blackwell shook their hands. "It's been a pleasure, Doctors."

"I can't thank you enough!" Cassie said.

"That goes for me too, sir," said Paul. "Without your help, we'd still be battling red tape. We really do appreciate your efforts on our behalf."

"There is one problem," the commander added. "Letting the wisents out of their crates wasn't very difficult, but getting them back in is going to be tricky." He laughed.

"I'll take care of it." Paul picked up his medical bag from the corner. "If you'll take me to the hangar, I can tranquilize them. We'll need some extra hands as well."

"You've got them." The commander strode to the door. "After you, Doctor."

Paul glanced at Cassie. "Do you think you can pack for both of us?"

"Sure," she agreed.

It didn't take long to get everything ready, since neither of them had really unpacked. As she was placing the last piece of luggage in the front room, Paul reappeared.

"How's it going?" he asked, frowning worriedly.

"We're all set. How are the animals?"

"The crates are already inside the C-130, strapped down. There's only one problem."

"What's that?"

"One more form needs to be signed, and the officer hasn't come with it yet."

"What should we do?"

"One of us is going to have to stay behind. Since the animals are primarily my responsibility, I'm going to take that flight out and monitor them throughout the trip. There's another transport leaving in a couple of hours."

Cassie was disappointed not to be able to return with him, but she tried not to let it show. She had so much to tell him, but it was too important to rush through. There would be time enough later. "All right. I'll stay behind and catch the next plane."

Paul gave her a warm smile. "Thanks." His eyes held hers for a brief eternity before he finally turned away. "I'll see you back at work the day after tomorrow."

"Day after?"

"You'll be spending most of tonight on the plane, so you'll probably want to sleep tomorrow. Get some rest, and I'll see you bright and early Wednesday morning."

She nodded. "Paul, I wanted to—"

"We better get going, Dr. Kelly," Jenkins interrupted, "or you'll miss your flight."

Paul gave her a worried look. "Is it important?"

"Yes, but don't worry about it. I'll talk to you later."

She watched him leave, waving good-bye as the car sped away. Their love would simply have to wait.

Cassie arrived home early Tuesday morning. Every muscle in her body ached. It was all she could do to stay awake long enough to wash and take off her clothes. She hadn't managed to sleep a wink during the trans-Atlantic flight, and the taxi ride home had just about finished her off.

She sighed. Seven o'clock. Normally by now she'd be up and getting ready for work. Today she just crawled between the sheets and fell into an exhausted sleep.

The shrill ring of the telephone woke her abruptly sometime later. Cassie bolted upright and, with a curse, picked up the receiver.

Paul's voice said, "Cassie, is that you?"

"Yes." She rubbed her eyes. "I meant to call you as soon as I got in, but I guess I fell asleep. What time is it?"

"Eight P.M."

She gasped. "I've slept for eleven hours! I don't believe it."

"Look, I hate to bother you, but we have an emergency. I'm going to need you in surgery. Can you meet me at the hospital?"

Instantly alert, she began reaching for her clothes. "The wisents?"

"No. They're both fine. It's Paco, a six-month-old llama. His keeper noticed a lump near his tail. The vets on duty examined him, discovered it was a perineal hernia, and performed corrective surgery."

"And it's become infected?" Cassie guessed.

"Worse. Paco ripped out the stitches."

"Wonderful. That near the tail, I would have expected an infection, or loose stitches due to the stress of the sphincter muscles. Are you sure he *ripped* them out?"

"Positive. I've got him sedated now, but he's a mess. I need to try to patch up what's left of the pelvic diaphragm. He did a pretty good job of tearing himself up."

"Okay. I'm on my way. Where can I find you?"

"I'll be in O.R. getting our patient prepped. How long will it take you to get here?"

"Twenty minutes."

"Try for ten, all right?"

She made it in fifteen. Using her key, she opened the back door leading to the hospital area and went directly to O.R.

Paul was clipping new hair growth from the llama's hind-quarters when she walked in. "The more I look at this," he said, "the worse it gets."

"How did you learn something was wrong? Usually our keepers are gone by six at the latest."

"One of the technicians came to the nursery to feed a baby orangutan and decided to tour the park before heading home. Good thing she did, too. She spotted Paco lying in a pool of blood."

Cassie finished scrubbing up and, with Paul's help, slipped on a pair of surgical gloves. She noticed a sterile towel draped over the table that read, "It's your move, Doc."

"Debbie's idea of comic relief," Paul explained.

Working smoothly together, they removed the few stitches that still remained and reopened Paco's wound. They identified ligatures and removed fatty tissue, then worked to repair the pelvic diaphragm, which prevented the intestines from pushing their way out.

Paul watched Cassie as she methodically sewed together the severed ends, working with skilled precision. "Forget it, Cassie," he said softly. "We're not going to be able to repair it completely. There's too much damage. Let's just make sure the sutures holding the hernial funnel are intact, and close. It may not be good as new, but it'll work."

"We could use a nylon mesh to form a 'diaphragm' of sorts," she suggested.

He considered her idea. "Okay, let's try it."

By the time they were ready to close, Cassie was exhausted yet exhilarated by the success of a job well done. After helping Paul place the animal in a large crate, she peeled off the gloves, tossed them into the trash, and washed up.

He joined her by the sink. "You're an extremely skilled surgeon, Cassie."

She smiled brightly. "Thanks. That means a lot to me, particularly coming from someone whose ability I respect so much."

Her compliment brought a wide smile to his face. "We're a mutual admiration society."

She captured his face between her hands and kissed him tenderly on the lips. "We have to talk, Doc. We still have a few things to clarify between us."

He nodded. "All right." He glanced at the llama sleeping peacefully inside the crate. "I'm going to take him home so I can keep an eye on him. I don't think he'll try to tear those wire stitches out, since they'll prick his mouth every time he gets near them, but you never know. Why don't you come to my place, have a drink, and relax."

"Sounds good."

Paul carried the crate outside and loaded it into the

back of the zoo's van. "How about driving back with me? It would help if one of us could monitor Paco while we're transporting."

"Sure. I'll ride with him." She climbed into the back of the van and made herself comfortable.

CHAPTER
Fourteen

PAUL KEPT HIS speed carefully under control to avoid jarring Paco. Cassie's nerves were tingling. The time had come to open her heart to Paul. She was ready to accept the love he had offered and ready to give hers in return. But unspeakable, numbing fear suddenly gripped her. What if he had changed his mind?

Paul pulled into the garage and carried the crate with the sleeping llama into the kitchen. He placed it in a corner where Paco wouldn't be disturbed. Burglar, apparently accustomed to all types of overnight guests, glanced at Paco with little interest and walked away.

Cassie opened the back door for him and watched as he bounded across the yard.

"Leave the door open so Burglar can come back when he's ready," Paul said. "Paco should sleep for hours, so we don't have to worry about him." Paul led the way into the den and poured a cognac for each of them. He sat beside her on the couch and raised his glass. "To a very good bit of surgery, Dr. Prentiss," he toasted.

She sipped the amber liquid, then placed her snifter on the coffee table. "I've been thinking about what you said, and examining the way I feel..." She paused, unable to find the right words. "What I'm trying to say is... You see, after we spoke by the pond, I knew I had to make a decision, a commitment... Oh!" She made a face. "Words! To hell with them. I'll just show you."

Not giving him a chance to reply, she cupped his face in her hands and met his lips with a fiery kiss that left little doubt about her feelings. "What I'm trying to say is that I love you, Paul."

His smile was as bright as a thousand suns. Then he feigned a casual attitude. "I know you love me," he said nonchalantly. "I always did. It's about time you admitted it."

Groaning, Cassie hit him squarely on the head with a pillow. "You weren't supposed to say *that*."

He easily deflected a second blow and released a burst of unrestrained laughter. "Tonight, Cassie Prentiss, I'm going to make love to you very thoroughly and very lingeringly. It's our night, Cassie. Let's make it a celebration of our future. A very intimate celebration." He murmured the words over her lips, then closed the gap between them.

His plundering kiss made her senses reel. Flames licked

her body as he invaded the intimate recesses of her mouth with an urgency that left her trembling with longing. She unbuttoned his shirt and pressed her palms against his powerful torso. She sensed a radiant maleness about him as he tasted her lips, gently asserting dominance over her with an ease that sent shock waves coursing through her whole body.

Tearing his mouth away from hers, he stood and offered her his hand. Cassie allowed him to pull her up. His head was bent in concentration as he unbuttoned her blouse and released her bra. His expression was intent as he flicked his tongue over the delicate hollow of her throat, then cupped her breasts in his hands, his thumbs expertly teasing the darkened centers to taut peaks.

He undressed her with exquisite slowness, taking delight in the soft flesh beneath his palms. Then with a groan, he lifted her into his arms and carried her to the bed. Against her breasts she could feel the rapid pounding of his heart. His mouth moved in her hair, over her eyelids, and down her throat as his hand roamed freely across her back, over her buttocks, and between her thighs. Desire pulsed hot and heavy at her very core, and she twisted in his arms, wanting more of him, all of him. His fingers continued their relentless quest, taking her from one pinnacle to another. As the last shudder of response faded, he released her and covered her lips once more with a gentle kiss.

Several minutes later, she stirred. "You've made love to me, my darling. Now it's time for me to make love to you."

She finished undressing him as if in a wondrous ritual, marveling at the perfection of his male form. Lying down on the bed, she pulled him back onto the soft mattress.

Her hands and mouth embarked on a joyous voyage of rediscovery. He inhaled sharply as she caressed him most intimately.

At last he pushed her firmly back against the pillows. He had little control left as he captured her lips with probing passion. His lean body drove downward, in an intense rhythm, consuming them both in a bright, blinding ecstasy.

Paul buried his face against Cassie's throat and pressed tiny kisses into the smooth, sweat-dampened hollows, murmuring words of love that meant nothing, yet everything.

Rational thought returned slowly. "I've never experienced such bliss . . . outside of an ice-cream store," she murmured, teasing him.

He looked at her in surprise and chuckled. "And think of the advantages. I don't melt in the summer heat."

She propped herself up on one elbow and ran a finger over his lips. "No, your melting temperature is reached by other means." She met his lazy grin with one of her own. "I could stay here with you for the rest of my life."

He wrapped his arms around her waist and pulled her over his chest. "Why don't you?"

Cassie studied him, wondering if he had just proposed . . . or propositioned her. She didn't really care which. Nestled in his arms, she drifted off to sleep.

The sound of Burglar's bark woke both of them. "Do you think Paco's up?" Cassie asked groggily. She opened one eye to see sunlight streaming through the window.

"I'd better check." As Paul retrieved his pants from the floor, Cassie tossed back the covers and put on his shirt.

"What do you know! That shirt looks better on you than it does on me." He regarded her appreciatively.

"Thanks." She grinned. "Now let's see about our patient."

Cassie followed him to the kitchen. Burglar was standing by the open back door. Paul muttered an oath, and she followed his gaze. The crate door was ajar—and the crate was empty!

"Oh, my God! Paco's escaped!" Cassie cried. "Do you think he's still in the yard?"

"If we're lucky." Paul hurried outside, barefooted, and investigated. Cassie followed. The sun was just rising, casting long shadows across the lawn.

"How could he have woken up so soon?" Paul muttered under his breath. "He should have slept for hours!"

Cassie checked her watch. "It's been hours, Paul. He's got to be out here someplace."

"Not necessarily." Paul walked over to the fence where an animal had obviously dug a hole under it.

"He did all that in his condition?" Cassie asked, incredulous.

"No, Burglar did. That's why I don't let him out when I'm not home. He loves to dig. Let's go back inside and call the police."

"Paul, we can't do that! The police might hurt Paco. They wouldn't have the foggiest idea what to do if they found him."

"But a civilian might be worse. Someone's likely to shoot him."

Dashing back inside, Cassie dressed while Paul called the sheriff's department and made his report. He met her in the living room.

"They're sending a couple of men who were already

in the area," he told her. "I wonder where Paco learned to open those crate doors. Better yet, I wonder why he bolted like he did."

"Maybe his stitches started to bother him. He couldn't pull them out, so he got restless."

The doorbell rang and Paul escorted two uniformed officers into the room. "This is my colleague, Dr. Prentiss." The men nodded and identified themselves as Officers Clay and Harris. Paul continued, "This llama is extremely valuable to the zoo. We reared him in the nursery, so he's almost tame."

"But you said he's hurt," Officer Clay pointed out. "Is there a chance he could become aggressive?"

"Well, he might bite if someone he doesn't know tries to handle him, but he won't attack. I'd like to ride along with you while you search, so we can maintain radio contact. Meanwhile, Dr. Prentiss should accompany Officer Harris. That way, once the animal is found, we'll arrive at the scene almost immediately to take care of him."

"My thoughts exactly, Doctor," the officer agreed. "How far do you think the llama can get in his present condition?"

Paul exchanged glances with Cassie. "It depends. My guess is he'll wander off toward the desert, tire easily, and hole up someplace."

"But there's really no telling in what direction he went?" Officer Harris questioned.

"Unfortunately, no," Cassie said.

"We'd better get going then," said Clay. "You can ride with me, Dr. Kelly."

One hour elapsed without any sign of the missing llama. Cassie sensed a growing restlessness on the part of Officer Harris, with whom she was riding, but she kept her eyes glued to the terrain outside the window.

The incoherent squawk of the radio diverted her attention. "Okay, Lieutenant," Clay responded. "I'll tell her." He turned to Cassie. "We have a problem. The television station got hold of the news. One crew is already making the rounds. Others are on the way." He shook his head. "Let's hope we can keep control of the situation. Otherwise, we're going to have all sorts of problems—from traffic jams to people capturing what will turn out to be their neighbors' livestock or pets."

Another agonizing hour passed before word came over the radio that a farmer had spotted Paco in his cornfield. Cassie's hopes rose at the news. Minutes later they met up with Paul at the side of a dirt road. Unfortunately, the press was already there.

Men with cameras followed Cassie as several officers tried to push back the sizable crowd. "The farmer's sure he saw our llama here?" Cassie questioned Paul.

"Yes, but it still won't be easy to find him. The cornfield itself isn't very large, but if he's gone beyond it and into the desert..." He shrugged. "There are arroyos and riverbeds that provide plenty of cover. Paco could hide out there for days."

"In his post-operative condition that animal's already considerably weakened. Can he stay outside for long and still survive?"

"Probably not, Cassie, but what can we do? We're working as fast as we can."

She glanced behind her. "There are a lot of people here. Maybe some would agree to help. We certainly could use the extra manpower."

Paul nodded. "I think you're right." He conferred with the officers and then addressed the crowd. "I'm Dr. Paul

Kelly from the city zoo. As you know, we're having a problem locating one of our llamas. We just did some emergency surgery on him, and we're afraid that in his weakened state, the animal could worsen rapidly. We'd appreciate all the help we can get. The only thing we ask is this: if you do spot Paco, don't attempt to capture him yourselves. You could literally frighten him to death. Just contact any one of the sheriff's officers, Dr. Prentiss"—he pointed to Cassie—"or me."

"Doc, a lot of us have CB's," said a lanky young man dressed in cowboy boots and a hat. "How about setting up a communications network?"

"That sounds fine. In fact, why don't you coordinate it?"

More camera crews approached. A reporter held a microphone out toward Paul. "Exactly how did this happen, Dr. Kelly?" he asked.

"The zoo doesn't have the funds to hire a full-time night-shift technician," Paul explained. "When we have an animal that needs to be checked every few hours, I usually take it home with me. But Paco, who was raised in our nursery, seems to have picked up a trick or two. One of them, apparently, was how to open the crate door. He followed my dog outside, found a hole under the fence, and slipped right through it."

"Is the animal in any immediate danger?"

"He's been raised in captivity, so he's not used to fending for himself. Also, because of his weakened post-surgical condition, it's important that we find him as quickly as possible."

The reporter turned to the camera and recapped Paul's comments. After the broadcast ended, the television crews joined the search effort.

Paul and Cassie entered the cornfield. "I sure hope

we find Paco soon," she muttered.

He reached for her hand and gave it a gentle squeeze. "We will. Just stay alert."

As the officers fanned out, Cassie spotted a set of tracks on a sandy path leading out into the desert. "Paul!"

He saw it, too. "Let's follow the tracks. If they're Paco's, he can't have gone much further, not in his condition. The terrain gets very rough once you pass that bend."

Cassie matched his steps. "You know, I never expected last night to end like this."

He chuckled softly. "Neither did I. It certainly put a damper on my morning plans. I was just about to ask you if—"

He was interrupted by a muffled shuffling. Paul stopped instantly and Cassie pointed straight ahead. Inching forward, they spotted Paco lying in a bed of dirt and leaves. He glanced up, unconcerned, then laid back down.

Paul approached him slowly. After checking to make sure the stitches were still in place, he picked the animal up in his arms and returned to Cassie. "He's fine, though I think he's more than just a little tired."

Cassie patted Paco's head gently. "We'd better tell the others we've found him."

On the way back, Paul remained silent. But at the sight of the crowd ahead, he stopped and turned to face her. "There's something I've been meaning to ask you all night. Cassie, will you . . ."

A reporter with a toothy smile stepped forward and shoved the microphone inches from Paul's face.

". . . marry me?"

Silence descended in a wave over the crowd. Cassie looked deep into Paul's eyes, then at the expectant crowd. Everyone seemed to be awaiting her answer. Not a sound could be heard, not a movement could be seen, as she opened her mouth to speak. For a brief moment she felt suspended in time. "Yes," she murmured.

Time, sound, and motion speeded up to normal again. As the reporter began talking into the microphone about the real-life romance unfolding before the cameras, an officer took the placid llama from Paul's arms. "I'll take him back to my patrol car, Doc. I have a feeling you're going to need both arms for something else," he hinted discreetly.

As the crowd buzzed around them, Paul turned to Cassie and pulled her gently behind a van and away from prying eyes. "I love you, Cassie Prentiss," he whispered. "I love you, and I want to spend the rest of my life with you." His lips closed over hers.

Cassie opened herself to his embrace, pressing against his lean body. Suddenly bright floodlights engulfed them. Paul tore his lips from hers and looked up as another television crew bore down on them. He groaned.

But as his eyes shifted back to Cassie's, a slow, arrogant grin came over his face. "Oh, what the hell!"

Pulling her back into his arms, he bent down and seared her lips with a deep, passionate kiss. Sighing, she closed her eyes and melted into his arms as a boisterous cheer rose from the excited crowd.

WHAT READERS SAY ABOUT
SECOND CHANCE AT LOVE BOOKS

"I can't begin to thank you for the many, many hours of pure bliss I have received from the wonderful SECOND CHANCE [AT LOVE] books. Everyone'I talk to lately has admitted their preference for SECOND CHANCE [AT LOVE] over all the other lines."
    —S. S., Phoenix, AZ*

"Hurrah for Berkley . . . the butterfly and its wonderful SECOND CHANCE AT LOVE."
    —G. B., Mount Prospect, IL*

"Thank you, thank you, thank you—I just had to write to let you know how much I love SECOND CHANCE AT LOVE . . . "
    —R. T., Abbeville, LA*

"It's so hard to wait 'til it's time for the next shipment . . . I hope your firm soon considers adding to the line."
    —P. D., Easton, PA*

"SECOND CHANCE AT LOVE is fantastic. I have been reading romances for as long as I can remember—and I enjoy SECOND CHANCE [AT LOVE] the best."
    —G. M., Quincy, IL*

*Names and addresses available upon request